W9-BZN-128

DISCARD

Hush-Hush

HUSH-HUSH

STUART WOODS

THORNDIKE PRESS
A part of Gale, a Cengage Company

GALE
A Cengage Company

Copyright © 2020 by Stuart Woods.
A Stone Barrington Novel.
Thorndike Press, a part of Gale, a Cengage Company.

ALL RIGHTS RESERVED
This is a work of fiction. Names, characters, places, and incidents either are the product of the author's imagination or are used fictitiously, and any resemblance to actual persons, living or dead, businesses, companies, events, or locales is entirely coincidental.
Thorndike Press® Large Print Basic.
The text of this Large Print edition is unabridged.
Other aspects of the book may vary from the original edition.
Set in 16 pt. Plantin.

LIBRARY OF CONGRESS CIP DATA ON FILE.
CATALOGUING IN PUBLICATION FOR THIS BOOK
IS AVAILABLE FROM THE LIBRARY OF CONGRESS.

ISBN-13: 978-1-4328-8042-2 (hardcover alk. paper)

Published in 2021 by arrangement with G. P. Putnam's Sons, an imprint of Penguin Publishing Group, a division of Penguin Random House LLC.

Printed in Mexico
Print Number: 03   Print Year: 2021

HUSH-HUSH

1

Stone Barrington awoke slowly on a Sunday morning. The evening before had been spent with his good friend Dino Bacchetti, and had involved good beef, good wine, and various spirits before and after dinner. Stone was alone in his bed, which was not his preference.

He was alone in his house, too, he recalled, since he had given his cook and house-keeper, Helene, and her husband, Fred Flicker, the weekend off. There was, he remembered, a housemaid stationed in the kitchen to meet his culinary needs. He picked up the phone and dialed an extension.

"Yes, sir?" an accented voice responded.

"This is Gilia."

Gilia was Greek, being one of a number of Helene's nieces who occasionally landed in his employ.

"Breakfast," he said huskily.

"Your usual, sir?" she asked.

"Yes, thank you."

"Only a little minutes," she replied.

"Good." He hung up.

Gilia had been taught well. The eggs were soft and creamy and properly salted, the sausages were tender and juicy, and his Wolferman's English muffin was perfectly toasted and buttered. By the time he had wolfed it all down, he felt restored. He was searching for an old movie to watch on TV and had just selected a John Wayne western, John Ford's *Rio Grande,* when his cell phone rang — the secure one. He picked it up. "Speak," he said. It was likely to be one of two people on the line; he hoped it was the tender gender one.

"What kind of greeting is that?" she asked.

"A cautious one," Stone replied. "I was hoping it was you and not Lance." Lance Cabot was the director of Central Intelligence, for whom Stone served as a special adviser. The woman on the line was the President of the United States, Holly Barker, with whom Stone had had an affectionate relationship for many years, off and on.

"I was thinking of coming to New York," she said. "When would be convenient for you?"

"How about right this minute?"

"You understand there are arrangements to be made."

"I thought we had that all ironed out and given a code name, 'Turtle Bay.' " That was the name of the neighborhood surrounding a private garden on which his house was located. "All you have to do is dial a number, speak those words, and you'll be here in time for lunch."

"I know that's supposed to be how it works," she said, "but I've never actually used it. And things have a way of going awry when their operation depends on the workings of the federal government."

"Oh, ye of little faith," Stone said, reprovingly.

"My faith in my government, or lack of same, is based on long experience."

"But your experience at the top of it is brief," he replied. "Try it and see."

"Hang," she said, picking up another phone and dialing an extension. She held the other phone so he could hear the conversation.

"Yes, Madam President," a male voice said after a single ring.

"Execute Turtle Bay," she said.

"Your helicopter will arrive in thirty minutes," he replied. "ETA, East Side

9

Heliport in one hour and forty-two minutes. Weather is favorable all the way. A three-car SUV group will greet and transport you to your destination."

"Excellent," she said, and hung up. "You get that?"

"I did. Sounds as if it should work as planned," he said. "Do you want to go out for dinner?"

"You know we can't appear in a New York restaurant without causing a press riot."

"Then I'll have you all to myself."

"You could invite the Bacchettis," she replied.

"Done."

"I'll look forward to that. Tell Viv I'm dressing to kill. See you soon."

Stone looked forward to it as well. He called another number.

"Bacchetti," a gruff voice replied.

"Which one?"

"The one who didn't have to go through menopause."

"Holly's on her way. Dinner here this evening?"

"Viv will want to know what we're wearing."

"You and I are wearing tuxedos. Tell Viv to let her imagination run wild."

"I can't do that. It would mean an all-afternoon shopping trip and a big dent in her credit card."

"*C'est la guerre,* pal. Six-thirty for drinks." He hung up. Then, as he did, he remembered that Helene was away for the weekend, and he was *not* cooking in a tuxedo, or out of one, for that matter. He called Fred's cell phone.

"Yes, sir?"

"I'm sorry to disturb you, Fred," Stone said, "but our friend Holly is coming to dinner, as well as the Bacchettis, and I don't know if Gilia can handle that."

"One moment, sir." He came back a moment later. "Helene says Gilia can manage with what's in the fridge and the pantry. She'll call her with instructions. Not to worry."

"Thank you, Fred," Stone said and hung up, feeling relieved.

Holly arrived with four pieces of luggage and one Secret Service agent, a woman named Midge. The other agents had to loiter in the garage or around the neighborhood.

She flung herself into his arms. "I want you," she said, "but I need a nap."

"You know where the bed is," he said, leaving Midge to get Holly's luggage aboard the elevator. Stone looked in his study for a book he had been reading but didn't find it; so he went downstairs to his law office and did. He was about to leave the room when there was a trumpet fanfare, and a message appeared on his desktop computer screen. Stone walked over, sat down, and read it.

Dear Sir,
Your computer, its hard disk, and all your programs and files are now frozen. Please understand that I have been reading them for weeks and, as a result, I know everything there is to know about you — your address and phone numbers, your social security number, your tax returns, and all your financial information are at my fingertips. I can dump your stock portfolio and deposit the funds in any bank account, anywhere. I can publish your tax returns in your local newspaper. I can print and distribute all the deeply personal e-mails you have sent to women over the years, some of them well-known to the public. In short, I can make your life a permanent hell.

But I am a reasonable person, and I will provide you with a means of avoiding these disclosures. All you have to do is

12

to purchase one million dollars' worth of Bitcoin on the Internet and transfer them to an account that I will provide details for later. Upon receipt, your files will be restored, your computer unlocked, and it will be as if you never had the pleasure of meeting me. You have until noon Friday next to accomplish this: if you should fail to meet that deadline, your life will lie in ruins.

There is a window at the bottom of your screen where you may send me an e-mail, should you wish.

Regards,
Dodger

Stone read it again, then pressed the Print Screen button and waited for the printer to spit out the copy. When it had done so, he typed GO FUCK YOURSELF into the e-mail window. Then he took his book upstairs and settled in to read.

2

It was the best kind of dinner: old friends, a comfortable atmosphere with a cheerful fire burning in the grate, and a dinner that was nearly as good as Helene's would have been. Afterward, the ladies excused themselves for a trip to the powder room. They might as well have been in London, Stone thought.

"What's new?" Dino asked.

Stone took a folded sheet of paper from an inside pocket and handed it to him. "This is new," he said.

Dino read it, twice. "Are your computers blocked?"

"Mine is. I didn't try Joan's."

"Are you going to pay the million bucks?"

"Of course not!" Stone said, with as much restraint as he could muster.

"You're pretty hot about this, then," Dino said, leaning back in his chair and sipping his cognac.

"Wouldn't you be?"

"Me? I would have already turned this over to our tech guys and forgotten about it."

"I don't have a tech staff on call," Stone said.

"Don't you? There's Bob Cantor; there's that kid, Huey, that you worked with on the *New York Times* thing. And of course, there's Lance Cabot, who has the tech world at his fingertips."

"Oh, them. Well, I guess I could call one of them."

"Call all of them," Dino advised. "Otherwise, you're going to find yourself with thousands of dollars' worth of useless computers. Oh, and then there's the scandal, if your attacker stumbles into your e-mails from Lance."

Stone took a big gulp of his cognac and swirled it around in his mouth before swallowing. "It's embarrassing," he said.

"I think Lance is going to find it more than embarrassing," Dino said. "He's been sending us all those reports from the field, along with the analyses."

Stone winced. "You're right. I'm going to have to call him."

"And then . . ." Dino said slowly, "there's Holly. I expect you have quite a few e-mails from her in an encrypted file."

Stone sucked his teeth and bathed them in brandy. "Thank God they're encrypted," he said.

"Your computer was encrypted, too," Dino pointed out. "And yet . . ."

The women returned in time to keep Stone from exploding.

"What's wrong?" Holly asked Stone.

"Wrong? Not a thing."

"I'm not buying that."

"And look at Dino," Viv said. "He's just scored some big point. So Stone's ox has probably been gored."

"We're not talking," Dino said smugly.

"Stone?" Holly said.

"Dino's not talking."

"Dino," Viv said, "you're going to tell me."

"If I feel like it," Dino replied airily.

"You may want to reconsider your position."

"It's Stone's problem. He can tell you, if he wants."

"It's something I'd rather keep to myself," Stone said firmly. "For the moment."

Later, Holly crawled into bed with Stone and slung a leg over his. "Are you sure you don't want to tell me?"

"I'll handle it myself," Stone replied, giving her a long kiss.

16

"You're trying to distract me from the subject?" she said.

Stone kissed her again and threw in a caress to a place she loved. "Is it working?"

It was working.

Stone arrived at his desk the following morning, approximately on time, and his secretary, Joan, knocked and came in. "We don't have any computers," she said. "Just black screens. Nothing works. Shall I call somebody?"

Stone thought about that: if he said no, he'd never hear the end of it. He handed her the sheet of paper.

She read it carefully. "There's nothing pertaining to you, explicitly. He doesn't use your name, address, or phone number. It's a scam. He sent out a zillion of these, and it's just a phishing expedition. Don't bite."

Stone said nothing.

"You bit," she said firmly.

"I only told him to go fuck himself."

"Hook, line, and sinker," she said.

"Hardly that."

"Now he knows you exist. Before, you were just a file name among millions he stole from some mailing list. And it never hurts not to be disrespectful. What's in it for you to piss him off?"

17

"You're exaggerating the problem," Stone said. "From now on, I'll just ignore him."

His computer made a rude buzzing noise, and he and Joan both looked at the screen.

Now, it's a million and a half.

Stone swung around and aimed for the keyboard. Joan took hold of his chair and held him back. "Don't, you'll just make it worse!"

"How could it be worse?" Stone asked.

"Well, he could be listening to our conversation."

Stone opened his mouth to speak, and he clapped a hand over it.

"Shush."

Stone nodded and removed his hand.

Joan whispered in his ear, "Call Lance."

3

Stone did not want to make this call. Every time he asked Lance Cabot for something, there were repercussions. Lance always wanted something in return, and it was usually more than he had given Stone, or more than Stone wanted to give him. He dialed the number.

"Good morning, Stone," Lance said in his silken baritone and New England accent.

"Good morning, Lance," Stone replied.

"What may the Central Intelligence Agency do for you this fine day?"

"I have a problem, one that involves the Agency, you specifically."

"I don't much like the sound of that," Lance said.

"Neither do I, but there it is."

"There what is?"

"There is an attempt at extortion, concerning the computer systems in my home and office."

"Let me guess. Someone claims to have made a movie of you masturbating to a porno movie."

"Not that one. No grounds."

"If you say so."

"I do say so."

"What then?"

"Someone has frozen my computers and threatens to destroy and expose their contents unless I pay him one and a half million dollars in Bitcoin."

"I don't see the problem," Lance said. "You surely have that many dollars to spare. Our investigation of your background shows that you do. Pay the extra two cents."

This was from an old Yiddish joke dating to the days of vaudeville, but Stone didn't bite. "If it were only two cents, I still wouldn't pay it."

"Oh, Stone, you choose the oddest times to become a man of principle. Why do I care what happens to your computers?"

"Because there are many communications and documents from you lodged on their hard drives," Stone said. "The man purports to have read all my important information, and one assumes this would include all those little love letters of yours and the details of a number of Agency operations, some of which may still be running."

20

Lance took a moment of silence for that to soak in. "We are not going to give your extortionist one and a half million dollars in Bitcoin," he said.

"As I've said, neither am I. So where does that leave us?"

"Where do you *think* it leaves us?" Lance snapped.

"It leaves you worse off than me."

This stopped Lance for a full ten seconds. "Are you threatening me, Stone?"

"No, an extortionist is threatening you — and, of course, me, as well."

"What do you propose I should do about this situation?"

"Well," Stone said. "Best case: you have your people track down the extortionist, destroy all his equipment, put his name on every conceivable watch list, which would keep him from finding this sort of work again. And, come to think of it, maybe slap him around a bit, just enough to give him a glimpse of his own blood."

"You've been watching too many Bruce Willis films," Lance said.

"No, I've been reading your ops reports. Now, have you a counterproposal for action?"

" 'Action this day,' " Lance muttered.

"Fine with me. I've got until noon Friday."

"I was quoting Winston Churchill," Lance said, "not making a suggestion. Churchill used to attach notes with those words to his orders. For a while everybody jumped, but after a little longer, people got used to them and ignored them."

"Is that happening to you, Lance? Are your people beginning to ignore you?"

"Not until after their resignations have been accepted."

"Let's go back to the beginning of this pinball game," Stone said. "I am not going to pay the extortionist a million and a half dollars in Bitcoin nor in quarters, dimes, nor pennies. Your turn."

Lance sighed. "All right, I'll send somebody around to your office."

"Thank you. Please stress to your man that he is being sent to restore my computers to their previous health, not to bowdlerize them and leave them in a smoking heap on my office floor."

"I'll try to remember," Lance said, then hung up.

Stone hung up, too, feeling let down. Somehow he had expected more of a cavalry charge than just a home visit. He looked at his watch; it was still running, and the time was eleven o'clock.

There was a knock at his door, and Holly

22

walked in, wearing a tailored suit and looking all business. "Good morning again," she said.

"Good morning. Are you off somewhere?"

"I am speaking at a luncheon given by the Foreign Policy Association, to which I have, mercifully, not invited you."

"How can I thank you enough?" he replied.

"I'll think of something," she replied. "We have one more night together before I flee."

"I've learned to take what I can get. What would you like for dinner?"

"Let's order in Chinese from that fabulous place you know. We can dine naked."

"Then the food hardly matters," he replied.

She gave him a wet kiss and left, headed for the garage.

Ten minutes later, Joan buzzed him. "Rocky, from Lance, to see you."

"Send him in."

Joan laughed and hung up. A moment later a young woman wearing slacks and a cashmere sweater entered his office. Stone particularly appreciated cashmere sweaters that were not marred by bras. "I'm Rocky Hardwick," she said. "Where's your computer?"

23

"I'm Stone Barrington," he replied, and pointed at his desk. "And that's my computer."

She set down a briefcase and a leather satchel. "Pardon me, as I change," she said, producing a pair of coveralls from the satchel and pulling them on over her clothes. "Get out of my way."

"I wasn't aware that computers are greasy," Stone said, rising from his desk and moving to a leather chair.

"You never know," Rocky said. She produced a fat laptop computer, unplugged a circuit board from Stone's computer, and used a cable to attach it to her laptop. "Now, let's have a look at your hard drive." She typed nonstop for about half a minute, then sat back and watched her screen.

The laptop uttered a *pfft* noise and went dark.

"What was that?" Stone asked.

"That was the sound of your attacker's bot destroying my computer's hard drive. At the very least." She packed up her tools and laptop.

"Where are you going?" Stone asked.

"This problem is going to require a trip to the lab," she said.

"In New York City, I hope."

"Yep."

"Are you going to be able to fix this?"

"That depends on your definition of 'fix,' " she replied.

"Cure, heal."

"Maybe. Bye-bye." She packed her boiler-suit and left.

Joan came in. "That was fast."

"It was that," Stone replied.

"Are we up and running?"

"Neither. Something on my hard drive attacked her computer. She's taking it to her lab."

"That's not encouraging," Joan said.

"No, it is not."

"Shall I start buying Bitcoin?"

"Not ever," Stone said.

"Then you have a plan?"

"I have the hope that Rocky has a plan," Stone said, "and as far as Bitcoin is concerned, I prefer my currency with pictures of American presidents on it. I don't trust zeros and ones."

"I'm with you, boss."

"That is so reassuring," Stone replied. "Now, go work without a computer."

"Well, let's see," she muttered. "I think I still have a typewriter around here somewhere."

Shortly, he could hear key tapping on an IBM Selectric.

25

4

They sat on the bed, eating pot stickers, shrimp balls, fried rice, sweet and sour chicken, and two or three other things.

"This is so great," Holly said. "I never get to eat like this in the White House."

"They don't have Chinese delivery in Washington?" Stone asked.

"Will Lee told me — and I didn't believe him — that he could never get a pizza delivered. By the time it passed through the X-ray and security inspections and they got it up to the family quarters, it would be cold, and he hated reheated pizza."

"It's just one of the human tragedies associated with being President of the United States, I guess."

She laughed. "At least they can't deny me sex in New York now and then."

"That raises a question: How are we going to handle it when we get caught?"

"Caught? You mean red-handed, like

somebody kicks in the door and photographs us in flagrante delicto?"

"No, they'd never get that far. But somebody is going to catch on eventually, maybe
very soon. Somebody will bribe a maid at
the Carlyle, who'll tell them you're not
sleeping there when you're in town. Then
they'll start working their way down the list
of your male acquaintances; pretty soon
they'll come to that photograph of us waltzing, and they'll give 'waltzing' a whole new
meaning. It's inevitable."

"I thought just death and taxes were
inevitable. They're adding screwing to the
list?"

"They'll add whatever they like to the
list," Stone said. "And screwing will be
number one."

"Well, I'll just have my press secretary an-
nounce, when it comes up, so to speak, that
the president will have no comment on her
personal life."

"You think that will satisfy them?"

"I don't much give a damn if it satisfies
them. I'm not in the business of satisfying
the press."

"Oh, no?"

"Well, not about my personal life, anyway."

"You're a brave woman."

"No, just randy."

"How do you satisfy that randiness when I'm not around?"

"Let's just say that you would love watching me."

"I bet I would, but I'd rather handle it myself."

"Well, you'd better start now," she said, "because if I eat much more Chinese food, I'm going to be incapable of participating."

They put away the chopsticks and moved the tray off the bed.

Stone kissed her goodbye in the garage. "Next week?" he asked hopefully.

"Not likely. You'll just have to trust me to do the best I can," she replied. Then she got into one of the three SUVs, and they drove out of the garage.

Stone went back to his office, dejected.

"There's a message from our extortionist," Joan said.

"What's the message?"

" 'Ticktock, ticktock.' "

"Where's what's-her-name?"

"Rocky Hardwick?"

"That's the one."

"She's on her way over."

"Is she on her way over with a solution, or just on her way over?"

"We'll soon learn."

■ ■ ■ ■

Rocky showed up in a different outfit, but still bra-less, to Stone's satisfaction. He liked that look; it helped him put Holly out of his mind.

"Okay," she said, "we were unable to restore your hard drive to health, but you haven't lost all your data. It's backed up on Joan's computer and on an external hard disk."

"Are you going to be as successful with those as you were with mine?" Stone asked.

"That remains to be seen," she replied. "Sometimes we fail."

"I'm sorry to hear that. Failure must be difficult for you."

Joan interrupted before Rocky could respond to that. "Right this way," she said.

Rocky picked up her briefcase and followed her out of the room, sticking her tongue out at Stone on her way.

Joan came back in. "I think this will go better if you don't make Rocky hate you," she said.

"Who, me? I'm the sweetest guy in the world!"

"Then find a way to prove it, before we permanently lose our ability to compute."

"I'll work on my manners."

"Always a good idea." She went back to her office.

Rocky came back into Stone's office. "Mind if I sit down?" she asked.

"Please," Stone said, waving her to the sofa. "You must be exhausted."

"Close."

"Would you like a drink?"

"Can you put your hands on a bottle of Scotch?"

"I can. Would you like a straw?"

"Just a little ice," she replied.

Stone poured them both a drink, then sat down at the other end of the sofa. They raised glasses and drank.

"Ahh, I feel human again."

"I'm glad," Stone said. "You certainly look human."

"Thank you for the kind word. Would you like to know how I did?"

"Love to."

"I've restored Joan's computer and the backup hard drive to health. I'll bring you a new computer tomorrow and transfer all your data. It will be like I was never here."

"I'm not sure I want it to be like that."

"You are sweet, when you're trying."

"Joan remarked on my lack of manners. I

apologize, I was just frustrated."

"Well, we wouldn't want you to feel that way, would we? Maybe some more good news would help."

"I love good news. Never get enough of it."

"We've located the computer from which your trouble originated."

"Is it right here in the city? Can I walk around the corner and slug the guy?"

"Not exactly. The coordinates put it about twelve miles southwest of Ames, Iowa."

"Have you called in a missile strike yet?"

"Not yet. We thought a personal visit might be more in order."

"Really?"

"Really."

"Can whoever visits him see that he will never type again?"

"First, we'll want to confiscate his equipment and question him."

"You have people in Ames, Iowa?"

"As a matter of fact, we have a team of two, working on a special project, in the computer sciences lab at Iowa State University. They're on their way, and someone will meet them at the location with a search warrant."

"Very efficient. I'm impressed." He snuck a look at her sweater. "More and more."

31

She laughed. "I'm flattered."

"It wasn't flattery," he replied, "just appreciation."

"That's even better," she said.

"Are you done for the day?"

"I'm just waiting on a phone call for the results of the home visit," she said.

"Let's wait in my study, it's more comfortable." He led the way upstairs.

5

Stone lit a fire and poured them another drink at the bar. "Do you have bars everywhere?" Rocky asked.

"Only where they're desperately needed," Stone replied. "One shouldn't have to hunt for a drink." He sat down next to her.

"Where are you from?" she asked.

"Less than an hour's walk from here, in the Village. You?"

"A small town in Georgia you've never heard of, called Delano."

"I've heard of it. What happened to your Georgia accent?"

"I was led astray by Yankee men and Englishmen."

"Englishmen?"

"I was stationed in London for four years."

"Ah. I love London."

"So do I."

"Why did you move?"

33

"One goes where the Agency tells one to go."

"I'll have to speak to the Agency about that."

"You must have a connection there, or I wouldn't be here working on your problem."

"I've been an Agency consultant for some time. Not long ago I got promoted to special adviser to the director. Sounds good, doesn't it?"

"It does."

"I think that's how Lance planned it. Doesn't mean a thing, though."

"It means you can call him when your computer needs fixing."

"I guess it does, at that. I'll have to drop him a note and thank him for sending you."

"More flattery."

"Whatever works," Stone replied.

Then her phone rang. "Yes?" She listened for a moment. "Just a minute, I'll put you on speaker so our client can hear." She pressed the appropriate button. "Can you hear us?"

"Sure."

"Go."

"Okay," a male voice said. "The site is a farmhouse, pretty much surrounded by an ocean of corn. We observed the place for a while to get a sense of who was home, and we saw only one person, male, six feet, a hundred thirty pounds, bad haircut. When we were pretty sure he was alone, we called in the SWAT team, searched the ground floor, then started up the stairs. He met us at the top."

"Was he armed?"

"With a Diet Coke," the man said. "We ascertained that it did not contain an explosive, then we served our warrant, searched him, then did the same with his computer installation."

"Describe his equipment."

"That's easy. He had a mini Mac, an eighteen-inch monitor, keyboard, and mouse."

"That's it?"

"No, he had a printer, too."

"How old is the subject?"

"Fourteen. He's a sophomore in high school. His dad teaches computer science at Iowa State; his mother teaches first grade. No siblings."

"What did you find on his computer?"

"We ran our diagnostics and found the same bot you found on the one in New York. Have you been able to trace it farther upstream?"

"As a matter of fact, we have, to a street address in Tallinn, in Estonia. If you want it raided, you're going to have to go upstairs for permission. That's it. We'll leave it to you to report our report."

She picked up the phone, took it off speaker mode, and asked him a few more questions. Then she said, "Bye-bye."

They both hung up.

"I was afraid of something like this," she said.

"Something like what?"

"The kid's computer was caught up in a search for computers with weak spots in their defenses. It was kidnapped by someone in Estonia and used as a relay to search other computers. And it found yours."

"Jesus."

"Well, yes. Now we'll trace back from the Estonian computer. It's my guess that the chain probably originates in Russia, from an intelligence agency like the GRU. Of course, it could originate in South Africa or Australia or anywhere else on earth, but the bot had certain characteristics that make us think it's of Russian origin."

"Sounds like I'm going to have to go a long way to punch this guy in the nose."

"Possibly. It could be someone who just wants us to *think* the source is Russian. Who knows?"

"So we're not going to find out who did

this or why?"

"Not unless someone higher up perceives this as a threat to the computers you've been communicating with at the Agency," she said. "Like Lance Cabot's computer. Don't worry, they'll be keeping an eye on it, and they'll let you know if that happens."

"You must be hungry," Stone said.

"Why do you think that?"

"Because *I'm* hungry."

"You're a good judge of character. Where shall we go? I'm not exactly dressed up."

"How about right here?" Stone asked. "What would you like?"

"What's on the menu?"

"Whatever you want. My cook, Helene, is very good at her native Greek cooking."

"Okay, I'll have something Greek."

Stone pressed a button, and Fred Flicker appeared in the doorway. "Good evening, sir."

"Good evening, Fred. This is Ms. Hardwick. Would you tell Helene we'd like something Greek for dinner, and in the meantime, some canapés, so we won't faint?"

"Of course, sir. And the wine?"

"You choose it."

Fred dematerialized.

"As easy as that, huh?"

"Fred is a wonder; so is Helene. They've been on holiday, so they should be refreshed."

They started with a Pâté Diana, duck's liver with lots of butter, then went on to dolmades — stuffed grape leaves — and other delicacies, with a bottle of Greek wine chosen by Fred.

"That was better than going out," Rocky said.

They moved back to the sofa for coffee and cognac, and Stone threw another log on the fire.

"I don't think I've ever felt so comfortable," Rocky said.

"Flattery."

She laughed. "Entirely in earnest." She took a deep breath and exhaled. "When do you make your move?"

"Move?"

"*That* move," she said.

"Oh, that one. How about next time we meet?"

"Sounds good. I'll remember not to overeat."

Later, Stone walked her down to the garage, and Fred drove her home.

"Next time," she called from the open window.

6

Stone Barrington sat at his desk on Friday morning, reading a contract on his computer. Joan buzzed him.

"What?"

"We have to get out," Joan said. "Right now."

"What are you talking about?"

"Getting out."

"At whose suggestion?"

"Rocky Hardwick, and it isn't a suggestion."

"What does she mean by 'get out'?"

"Of the office. She said to go into the garage and take your laptop with you. Me, too."

"Are you taking this seriously?" Stone asked.

"Pretty much. I'm in the garage. Join me? You've got less than a minute." She hung up.

Stone looked at his wristwatch; nearly

twelve. Suddenly, it came to him. He grabbed his coat, his briefcase, and his laptop, and ran for it. He had just closed the garage door when there was a dull thud from the direction of his office. He looked around for Joan; she was cowering with Bob behind the Bentley.

"Did you hear that?" she said.

"Of course I heard it. Felt it, too."

His cell phone rang. "Yes?"

"Did you get out in time?" It was Rocky.

"Yes. What happened?"

"Well, I was going over the report about your computer from my colleague at the lab, who noticed the computer smelled a little of motor oil. They only mentioned it because it seemed odd. But I knew that to be a scent consistent with C-4."

"Is it safe to go back in there?" he asked.

"I think you'd better let our bomb people go in first."

"You have bomb people?"

"Of course."

"Well, send 'em over."

"You stay in the garage until they give you the all clear."

They both hung up.

Stone and Joan sat in the Bentley, listening to jazz on the radio, until someone hammered on the garage door.

Stone rolled down the window. "Come in!" he yelled.

The door opened and a man in a jumpsuit, carrying a toolbox, walked in. "All clear," he said, beckoning them.

As Stone walked into his office Rocky was entering through the street door. "Everybody okay?"

"Everybody but my office," Stone said, looking around.

"It's not so bad," Joan said. "Mostly broken glass and, of course, broken computer."

"We need to go over the place again and be sure that the only bomb was in the computer."

"You two come with me," Stone said to Joan and Rocky. He led them to the kitchen where Helene made them smoked salmon sandwiches, and Stone opened a bottle of chardonnay.

"Sorry about that," Rocky said.

"You don't need to be sorry. You got us out in time," Stone replied. "Tell me, why did you call Joan, instead of me?"

"Because I didn't want an argument."

"An argument?"

"You're not the kind of person to just act immediately on a warning. You'd want a full explanation of what was happening, and by the time I finished telling you, you'd have been missing a hand or two."

"I like my hands where they are," Joan said, "at the end of each arm. I got the hell out."

"And you finally called me," Stone pointed out.

"And in plenty of time, too," she said.

"I wouldn't call less than a minute plenty of time."

"It was enough."

Stone had to admit she was right. "Well, thank you both for the parts you played in keeping us all safe."

"What makes you think we're safe?" Joan asked.

Rocky broke in. "I think it's very likely that you're safe," she said.

"I'm sorry," Joan said, "but 'very likely' safe isn't safe enough for me."

"By the time my people finish up, you'll be very safe," Rocky replied. "They're very good at what they do."

"How good?" Joan asked.

"May I point out that they're still alive?"

"Good point."

"What about the kid in Iowa?" Stone asked.

"He was at school, and his parents were

at work. I'll call later and find out if there was an explosion."

"Did my computer blow up?" Joan asked.

"No, I saw it on the way in, and it was intact. The boys are checking it out to be sure."

As if on cue, the boys entered the kitchen. "All clear," one of them said. "The other computer and the backup hard drive weren't wired to explode."

"You fellas sit down and have a sandwich," Stone said. "I want to survey the damage again." He got up and walked back to his office, followed by Joan and Rocky. He looked around. "Joan?"

"Yes, sir?"

"Buy me a new computer and have Rocky bulletproof it. Then you and Helene clean this place up."

"I'll stop by tomorrow and download all the data from Joan's computer to yours, then you'll be back where you were," Rocky said.

"Rocky, come with me, please."

He led her out of the office and to the elevator. "I didn't give you the house tour the other evening," he said.

"No. I guessed there was a bedroom some-where."

He led her into the master suite. "Your

43

suspicions were justified." He took her face in his hands and kissed her. "I couldn't think of a better way to thank you," he said.

She put her arms around his neck. "I can think of a better way," she said, kissing him back. "And I believe I'm getting a favorable response."

"You are, indeed," Stone said, kicking the door closed.

"Will we be undisturbed here?"

"Yes, unless there's another explosion."

They began working on each other's buttons.

They were at it for a half hour, then took a break.

"You're welcome," Rocky said.

"I felt welcome."

"You feel better than welcome," she said, fondling him. That led to another half hour of effort, this time more slowly and thoughtfully.

They napped for a while, then Rocky moseyed around the master suite, naked. "This has everything you need," she said approvingly.

"That's a perfect way of putting it," Stone agreed.

"I like the way you look naked," she said.

"Same here," he replied.

"I don't know if I'm up for another round."

"Thank God. Why don't we keep that for after dinner?" Stone replied. "I'll ask some friends to join us, if that's all right."

"For dinner, but not bed," she said.

"That was my thought."

"I like the way you think."

7

On the way to dinner, Stone explained about the Bacchettis — Dino and Viv. "Dino and I were cops together, and partners. He stuck with it, and now he's the police commissioner. Viv was a detective, but she retired when she married Dino."

They met at Patroon, a favorite restaurant of Stone and the Bacchettis. The owner, Ken Aretsky, sent over drinks and, after they had ordered dinner, a bottle of wine.

Viv bored in. "What do you do, Rocky?"

"I work for the government, in computer science."

"What sort of background do you need for that?"

"For me, a master's in the subject at MIT and a few years in the lab, a sort of internship, you could say."

"Does your work include defusing bombs?"

"No, when I run into something like that

I call somebody else, who does that kind of work and who, if he's lucky, still has all his fingers."

"Dare I ask what government agency you work for?" Viv dared.

"It's okay, Rocky," Stone said, "Dino is a consultant to the Agency, too, and anything he knows, Viv learns five minutes later."

"The CIA," Rocky replied.

"So you know Lance Cabot?" Viv persisted.

"We've met, but I work in the New York station, so I don't often bump into him in the hallways."

"If you did, would Lance know who you were?"

"He did the last time we met, but I can't vouch for his memory."

"Okay, Viv," Stone said, "if you keep going you'll end up in jail for espionage."

"When does nosy turn into espionage?" Viv demanded.

"About where you are now."

Viv changed the subject. "Where did you get that lovely diamond necklace?"

"I stole it, while on an assignment."

Viv's mouth dropped open.

"Rocky," Stone said, "if you keep answering Viv's questions, *you're* going to end up in jail."

47

"Oh, all right," Rocky said, "I got it from a man, which was pretty much the same thing as stealing it."

Viv managed a laugh.

"What do you do, Viv?"

"I'm chief operating officer of Strategic Services."

"The second largest security company in the world," Rocky said, nodding. "I've heard good things about their work."

"If you ever get tired of government work, come see me," Viv said, sliding her card across the table.

"Now this has gone from an interrogation to a job interview," Dino said.

Rocky tucked the card where her bra would have been, if she wore one. "I'll call when that happens," she said, ignoring Dino.

Dinner arrived.

"Interview concluded," Stone said, "dining now to begin."

They tucked in and ate voraciously without ever stopping talking.

"Why do you think this extortionist picked Stone?" Dino asked Rocky.

"People like this have two broad categories of victims: One, they send thousands of such e-mails to those on a list of wealthy

48

people, such as subscribers to some financial magazines. Two, they read something about the potential victim that makes him look like an attractive target, and go from there. Stone might look like a particularly interesting target if they've established a link between him and an intelligence service. I'm inclined to think the second category for Stone."

"Why?"

"Because they wouldn't go to the extreme of killing or maiming some ordinary civilian. That sort of action they would reserve for the connected. They want to be taken seriously, for next time."

"Why do you think there'll be a next time?" Viv asked.

"Because it's what they do for a living, and they probably do very well at it."

"Are they likely to come back at me, physically?" Stone asked.

" 'One never knows, do one?' as a great man used to say."

"I'm impressed that you know who Fats Waller is," Stone replied.

"Doesn't everybody?"

"Not everybody of your youth," he replied.

"I think you'll be gratified to know that your extortionist has committed a serious tactical error in trying to harm you. He and

49

his accomplices are now on a list of people sought by the Agency. If anything pops up anywhere in the world that even vaguely resembles the attack on you, the Agency will be all over it, and we never give up."

"That's comforting to know," Stone said. "I hope these people are aware of the Agency's attitude."

"If they're not, they soon will be," Rocky replied.

They were on dessert when Rocky's phone rang. "Excuse me, I'd better take this.

"Go," she said into the phone, then she listened for about a minute. "Take a look around, then reset." She hung up. "Your security system says that someone tried to enter your house without a key through the kitchen door to the garden."

"Is there anything I should do?" Stone asked.

"No, they're doing it. If they don't find a culprit, they'll reset the system, and that should be it."

"I hope so," Stone said.

"You should know that, while the monitoring of your system used to be done by a commercial service, it is now monitored by an Agency facility in the city, which will be much more attentive to your needs."

"I hope they haven't installed cameras," Viv said wryly.

Back at the house, they walked around and checked out things. "All seems well," Stone said.

"If all wasn't well, my people would still be here, rummaging around."

"And planting cameras?"

"Let's go upstairs and check," she said.

Rocky stood in the center of the master suite and looked around. "Nothing here that I can see."

"Is it possible that there is something here that you can't see?"

Rocky produced her cell phone and tapped on an app. "Nothing here," she replied.

"I want an app like that," Stone said.

"I'll set up your phone for that tomorrow," Rocky said.

"Will you stay the night?"

"Is there somewhere a girl can rinse out a few things?"

"There's a mini-combo washer/dryer in a cupboard in your dressing room, and a pop-out ironing board, too. But my recollection is that all you have to rinse out is a thong."

She smiled. "I'd like to rinse out my

51

blouse, too," she said, starting to unbutton. Stone helped as much as he could.

8

Stone and Rocky were reading the *Times* the following morning when his cell phone rang, caller unknown.

"Yes, Lance?" Stone said.

"I'm the only person who blocks calls, right?"

"To this number, yes."

"May I speak to Rocky, please?"

"Just a minute, I'll have to do a search for her."

"Just turn your head to the right and say, 'It's for you.' "

Stone handed the phone to Rocky.

She pressed the speaker button. "Yes, Director?"

"Are you enjoying your work?" Lance asked.

"Always, sir."

"I think that, given recent events, you should perhaps spend a good deal more time in Mr. Barrington's company."

"That's okay with Mr. Barrington," Stone said.

"No one cares, Stone. Rocky, messaged received?"

"Received and understood, sir. You can count on me." They hung up.

"You know Lance better than you admitted to Viv, don't you?" Stone asked her.

"I usually lie to people who are interrogating me. It's part of my training."

"What part?"

"Lying 101," she replied.

"Have you been lying to me?"

"About what?"

"Anything."

"No, you haven't interrogated me, so it hasn't been necessary."

"But you would lie to me, if you thought it necessary."

"Of course not," she replied. "That would be a violation of our personal relationship."

"Are you lying to me now?"

"Maybe."

"How can I tell?"

"You can't. I'm trained, remember?"

"I'd rather you didn't lie to me — ever."

"And I'd rather you didn't make it necessary for me to lie to you."

"Forget it."

"I'll try, but that may be a lie."

54

"So you won't forget it?"

"I don't forget much."

"Try."

"Forgetting is an involuntary act."

"This is a losing game, isn't it?" he asked.

"Probably."

He placed his hand in a tender place and wiggled his fingers. "Do you like this?"

"Oh, yes."

"Is that a lie?"

"Probably not."

"When can I trust you not to lie?"

"When I'm not lying."

"And when don't you lie?"

"At times like this," she said, squeezing his fingertips and kissing him on the top of his head. "You know what I like about you?"

"No, what?"

"Your constant readiness."

"That's flattering."

"No, it's just a fact." She pulled him on top of her. "And I'm not lying."

After lunch, Stone suggested a trip to Bloomingdale's.

"Why Bloomingdale's?" Rocky asked.

"Because I buy my boxer shorts there, and my stock's elastic is beginning to fail."

"On all of them?"

55

"Just the ones that I bought at the same time."

"Do I have to watch?"

"No, you can mosey around other parts of the store while I decide between plaids and stripes."

Stone thought he would lose her as they passed through the cosmetics counters, but she stayed at his elbow, even while he was deciding between plaids and stripes. He gave the clerk his credit card and adjusted the small mirror used for fitting sunglasses, which were displayed nearby. "Rocky?"

"Yes?"

"Do you think Lance would have us followed at Bloomingdale's?"

"I wouldn't think that Lance would care so much about your boxer shorts."

"I'm going to move over a foot or two; when I do, check the image in the mirror and tell me if you think the couple in neckties is following us. She's pretending not to like the tie he's chosen." He moved over, and Rocky replaced him in front of the mirror.

"Well?"

"I think they very well could be following us," she replied. "And if they are, I would tend to believe that Lance sent them."

"How certain is 'very well could be'?"

"Let's say I'm quite certain about it."

"What about the couple makes you so sure?" he asked.

"Well, for a start, I think she actually likes the necktie she's complaining about."

"Really?"

"Her heart isn't in it. Wives are never iffy about these things."

"Any other reason you're so sure?"

"There is the fact that the woman and I were in the same class at the Farm," she said, referring to Camp Peary, where CIA recruits undergo their initial training.

"That reason makes an impression."

"I'm impressed, too, that you spotted them when I didn't," Rocky said. "How did you do that?"

"I, too, thought her heart wasn't in the argument over the tie."

"Let's rumble them," Rocky said. "Follow my lead."

Rocky turned around and fixed the couple with her gaze.

"Betty!" she called out. "Did you see her jump at the sound of her name?" she asked Stone.

"I did, but she's ignoring you."

"Betty Swenson!" Rocky nearly shouted.

This time the woman turned and regarded Rocky, her eyebrows up. "Why, Rocky," she

57

said, managing to sound surprised.

"Let's go," Rocky said to Stone, then she walked toward the couple, while Stone trailed her.

Rocky offered her hand to shake, and Betty took it. "You look just the same," Rocky said.

"You look even better," Betty reposted.

"Who's this?" Rocky asked, turning to regard Betty's companion.

"This is my friend, Evan," she replied.

"Rocky Hardwick," Rocky said, shaking his hand. "And this is my friend, Stone Barrington," she said, "as if you didn't know."

Betty looked Stone over and decided to shake his hand. "How do you do, Mr. Barrington? And, Rocky, how would I know?"

"Because Lance told you. Stone, you see, is a senior adviser to Lance."

"Come to think of it, I believe I've heard the name. And you'll be glad to know, Stone, it wasn't taken in vain."

"Whether I would be glad of that depends on who spoke it," Stone replied.

"Tricky, isn't he?" Betty asked.

"Fairly," Rocky replied.

"Only fairly?" Stone asked, looking hurt.

"Don't worry, it's Betty who's being

58

tricky. Tell me, Betty, why would Lance assign someone I know to follow me?"

"Perhaps he thought you wouldn't blow me on sight," Betty replied. "Or perhaps, it's Stone we were asked to follow."

"Why would Lance want me followed?" Stone asked, innocently.

"Let me put it this way," Betty said, "we're both armed, and there are two more of us you haven't spotted yet. It was Stone who spotted us, Rocky, wasn't it?"

"Maybe," Rocky replied. "We're going to back off now and let you carry out your assignment."

"Oh, good," Betty said, beaming. She shook both their hands, and the couple wandered off toward a cash register, with a fistful of neckties.

"I don't get it," Stone said.

"There's already been one attempt on your life, Stone," Rocky said. "Betty was right, I shouldn't have blown her." She took his hand. "Let's go collect your boxer shorts."

9

They settled into a cab, and Stone told the driver to take them to East Seventy-second and Madison Avenue.

"Well, that was embarrassing," Rocky said.

"I embarrassed you?"

"No, you were just aware of your surroundings, and I wasn't — not sufficiently. Why did we go to Bloomingdale's for Polo boxer shorts when we were going to the Ralph Lauren store anyway?"

"I wanted to be sure of getting the ones I wanted, not the ones they wanted me to have."

"All right, I'll accept that."

"Do you really think the thing with my computer was an attack on my life, not the life of the hard disk?"

"Oh, that, too, but there was about an ounce of C-4 explosive in that bang, which could have taken your head off, if you'd been working at that computer. There's also

60

the fact that one cannot transmit explosives over the Internet, only trigger what has already been placed there."

"You mean someone was in my house at some point?"

"At some point, yes. The C-4 didn't arrive by homing pigeon."

"And no amateur could have breached my security system without setting off alarms."

"I wasn't going to bring that up, but yes."

The cab arrived, and they got out. Stone held the heavy store door open for her.

"What are we looking for?" Rocky asked.

"Tell you what: I'll look around for something to look for, and you look out for assassins."

"That's a sensible division of labor," she replied. "All I have to do is not confuse the assassins with the other two members of Betty's team, who will have changed places with her and her friend, Evan, taking the lead."

"What are the chances you would know one of them?"

"Poor."

"Lance wouldn't make the same mistake twice?"

"Lance didn't make it the first time," Rocky replied. "He would have instructed somebody, who would have instructed somebody. That last guy is who will burn, if this gets back to Lance."

"Life is complicated in the CIA, isn't it?"

"Not necessarily. I've already spotted the other team guarding you."

"Dare I ask?"

"Don't look now, but it's the gay couple looking at antique wristwatches near the front door, and there are two more, the women checking out the cabinet near the elevator, waiting to see if we get on."

"I could never be a spy," Stone said. "I wouldn't have spotted any of them."

"You just haven't been trained to the right level of paranoia," Rocky said. "After today, everybody you see will look like an assassin."

Stone laughed. "Forever?"

"No, just until the feeling of threat wears off. For a pro, it's forever. You can count on me for the paranoia."

"Let's look at shoes," Stone said, steering her past the elevators.

"Why would you ever want to? I've seen your dressing room, and the shoe rack is chock-full."

"I'm always on the lookout for a bargain," Stone said, checking out the shelves.

"Define 'bargain.'"

"Alligator shoes, half off. I couldn't pass

that up."

"I've seen your financial statement, Stone," she said. "If you want alligator shoes, why don't you just buy them?"

"Where's the fun in that?" Stone asked. "Your problem is that you're too wrapped up in looking for assassins to see the bargains."

"Thank God one of us is."

Stone spied a pair of alligator loafers, on sale. "Aha!"

Rocky jumped. "Don't do that."

"What?"

" 'Aha!' I thought you had spotted assassins."

"I'm much more focused than that," Stone said, picking up a loafer and stroking it. "In a 10D?" Stone said to the salesclerk.

"I'll check," the man said, then vanished through a small door.

Stone eased into an easy chair. "I'll cover the door from here," he said.

"And what am I supposed to do? Shop for shoes?"

"If you spot a bargain, sing out."

The salesclerk reappeared with two shoeboxes. "One black, one cognac," he said.

Stone tried on the left shoe of both of them in succession.

"Why are you trying on just the left shoe?"

Rocky asked.

"My left foot is slightly larger than my right. If they fit the left, they'll fit both. It's a time-saver." He turned to the clerk. "How about seventy percent off, if I buy both pairs?"

"I'll check with my manager," he said, and disappeared again through the small door.

"You're bargaining with them?"

"I'll bet it works, too."

The clerk came back. "Sixty percent off for both pairs."

"Done," Stone said, handing him the shoes. The clerk went away to bag them. "See that? I saved, what? A little more than thirteen hundred dollars."

"No, you spent nearly a thousand."

"Small minds quibble."

"I'm not quibbling. It's not my money."

"Good thing, too; I'd be running out of alligator shoes. Spot any assassins?"

"Only one candidate," Rocky said. "Just got off the elevator from downstairs."

"The only thing downstairs is the toilets."

"Assassins pee, too," she said.

"The guy dressed all in black, with a black hat over a billiard-ball head? Isn't he too obvious?"

"That doesn't mean you're safe," she replied.

The salesclerk returned with Stone's card and the receipt; he signed it.

"Can we get out of here?" she asked. "He could have one or more accomplices."

"I'm done," Stone said, rising. "Where are your four helpers?"

"I don't know."

"I guess the guy isn't obvious enough for them."

"Apparently not," she said, striking out for the front door. The doorman saw them coming and went outside to corral a cab. It was there when they arrived, and Stone tipped the doorman fifty dollars.

"That was very generous, wasn't it?" Rocky said as the cab pulled away."

"He may have saved my life," Stone said, looking back. "Our assassin is looking for his own cab, with no help from the doorman."

"You got yourself another bargain," Rocky said.

10

As they approached the house, Stone used his iPhone to open the garage door, dazzling the cabdriver.

"That never happened before," the man said.

"And may never again," Stone said, helping Rocky out of the cab. He tipped the man fifty, and the cab backed out of the garage. Stone closed the door behind him.

"Is fifty dollars your standard tip?" Rocky asked.

"Only when my life is at stake," Stone said, letting them into the house. "Where would you like to have dinner tonight?"

"Can I choose anyplace I like?"

"Of course."

"I choose, Brasserie Lipp."

"That's in Paris."

"That's the main reason I chose it," she said, "but I do like the *choucroute*. Also, Lance has suggested we get out of town, and as far away as possible."

Stone checked his watch. "I'm afraid I don't have a rocket ship at my disposal, so it'll have to be tomorrow night." He sat her down in the study with a drink, whipped out his cell phone, and called Brasserie Lipp, conducting a brief conversation in his schoolboy French. He hung up. "Tomorrow at eight."

"Don't we need to call an airline, too?"

"I thought you read my file."

"I missed the part about the jet fighter."

"Just an ordinary Gulfstream 500."

"Hotel?"

"House."

"I've underestimated you."

"You go right on doing that." He buzzed Joan.

"Yes, sir?"

"Let Faith know we're flying to Paris tomorrow morning, wheels up at eight AM; let Fred know, too." He hung up.

"Let me handle the transport on the other end. And I'll need to pack."

"Shop in Paris, instead of packing in New York. On me. You can handle the transport."

"Where's your house in Paris?"

"Quite near Lipp. Only yards from Ralph Lauren. His stuff suits you."

"Not often enough," she said.

"Clearly, you've been hanging out with the wrong men."

"Indubitably," she said. "How will I ever repay you?"

"Surprise me."

After dinner, she surprised him.

The following morning the Bentley disgorged them at the foot of the airstairs door of the G-500. An engine started as they climbed the stairs; once inside a stewardess closed and locked the airplane's door. Then the second engine started.

Twenty minutes after takeoff the airplane leveled off at flight level 510, and breakfast appeared before them, along with mimosas.

"Is it too early for you?" Stone asked, hoisting one.

"Certainly not," she said, joining him.

A half hour later the stewardess appeared and took away their dishes. "Faith says to tell you we'll have a 160-knot tailwind for most of the flight. We should land at six PM, local."

"You'll have time to choose a frock for dinner," Stone said, settling in with the *Times*. By the time he had finished the crossword, Rocky was dozing, and she didn't wake up until the landing gear came down at Orly, where general aviation flights had landed since the advent of Charles de Gaulle Airport.

Rocky looked around. "Are we there yet?"

"We will be in around two minutes," he said. Shortly, Faith landed smoothly, then was met by a truck with a flashing light and a sign that read: follow me. She did.

"Is Faith the pilot?" Rocky asked.

"Good guess."

"Do you always fly with the same crew?"

"No, Faith, the captain, is on staff. She hires whoever she needs for our flights from a list of qualified people."

The airplane stopped, and the engines wound down, then then it started to move again. "We're being towed into a hangar," Stone said.

"All part of the security arrangements," Rocky replied.

The airplane stopped, the stewardess opened the door and lowered the stairs, and a man bounded into the cabin.

"Rick!" Stone said, surprised. He pumped the man's hand. "Rocky, this is Rick La Rose, your chief of station in Paris."

"I know," Rocky said, shaking his hand.

"She arranged all this," Rick said. "You'll ride into the city with me, in a special vehicle."

"Rocky will be so pleased," Stone said.

"She's terribly concerned about assassins."

"And well she should be," Rick said.

The vehicle they entered reminded Stone of the ones Holly rode around in. Then he pushed Holly out of his mind.

Somehow, their driver had a remote control for the giant oaken doors that guarded the mews where Stone's house lay. Before they entered, Stone pointed out the Ralph Lauren store for Rocky's benefit, then they got out at the house.

He handed her a credit card. "May I carry your handbag for you?" Stone asked, in the absence of luggage.

"Thanks, I can manage. I'll scratch on your door in time to change for dinner."

"I can push it back to eight-thirty," Stone suggested, handing her a house key.

"Good idea." She departed through the small door in the big doors.

At eight o'clock, Stone was having a drink by the fireplace in his small study/library, when Rocky was escorted in by Marie, the housekeeper and cook, wearing a knockout dress and bearing many shopping bags. "I thought as long as I was trying it on, I'd just keep it on," she said.

"Well chosen," he said. "I can't wait to see you without it."

Marie helped her upstairs and showed her around the master suite.

They strolled down the Boulevard Saint-Germain to Brasserie Lipp. They were warmly greeted by the maître d' and seated with their backs to the mirror in the main dining room.

"I usually get sent upstairs, with the tourists," Rocky said.

"Once again, poor choice of male companions."

"I like being in front of the mirror," she said. "Whenever someone interesting comes in I can see them checking themselves out over my shoulder."

"It's true. How many of these diners are my bodyguards?" he asked.

"Don't ask. You'd never spot them anyway."

"I pick the two priests dining together over there."

"Don't be ridiculous. We can't involve apparent priests in gunfights in chic Paris restaurants. Lance is a Catholic, you know."

"I didn't know that Lance was swayed by any religious inclination."

"I didn't say he was swayed, but there's some tiny part of his brain stem that harbors a fear of messing with the Church."

71

"Good to know."

"Why?"

"Just good to know. The only bad information is no information."

"I like that," she said. "Can I use it?"

"As long as you credit me. I'm a lawyer, you know, and litigious, especially in matters of intellectual property."

"Well, if you're going to elevate everything you say to the level of intellectual property, I won't quote you at all. I'll paraphrase."

"You sound like a lawyer."

"It's the company."

They ordered the *choucroute,* a plate full of sliced, boiled meats and potatoes on a bed of sauerkraut.

"If I finish this, I won't be able to wear this dress," Rocky said.

"My diet is to eat half of everything I'm given," Stone said. "Make your eyes smaller."

"Even if I squint, it's still a lot of food."

They managed. Halfway through the *choucroute,* Rick La Rose walked in and, unescorted, sat down at a table directly across the room from them. The maître d' did not shout at him.

"He has a good field of fire," Stone said.

"I would expect no less of Rick," she replied.

"Doesn't it bother you that you're sitting cheek by jowl with somebody who, at any moment, could become the object of a fatal attack?"

"Nobody is trying to kill me," she said. "I just keep an eye on the other diners, as you may observe Rick doing."

Stone observed Rick doing just that. "I feel so safe," he said.

11

Stone woke the following morning to the absence of Rocky from his bed and the sound of the shower, mixed with the sound of steady rain outside, along with an occasional rumble and flash of lightning. He glanced at his watch: just past ten AM. He fumbled for his phone, called the Ralph Lauren store and asked for the manager, who knew him.

"*Bonjour, Monsieur* Barrington," the woman said.

"*Bonjour.* Do you recall a woman shopping with my credit card yesterday?"

"Of course."

"Last night, as I passed the shop, I saw a very handsome trench coat on a mannequin. Do you have that in the young lady's size?"

"One moment, please." She put him on hold, then came back directly. "Yes, we have it, Mr. Barrington."

"Would you please wrap it in a box with a big bow on it and deliver it to my home in the mews as soon as possible? And choose a suitable umbrella to go with it."

"Of course, Mr. Barrington. In thirty minutes."

Stone hung up. A half hour later, when Rocky came out of the shower, the box was on the bed.

"Have you looked outside? It's pouring."

"It does that in Paris, from time to time."

"What's this?" she asked, poking the box with a finger.

"A gift appropriate to the occasion."

"Do you always shop from bed?"

"Whenever possible. Open it."

In an instant she was shaking out the folded trench coat. "Oh! The perfect thing. And the umbrella matches the lining!" She put on the coat and modeled it for him. "It's perfect."

"I prefer you out of it," he said. She shook it off and went to him.

Later, when they had had breakfast and each other, she said, "Let's have a test of how observant you were last night."

"Okay, shoot."

"During the evening we saw someone we had seen before. Who was it?"

75

"Rick La Rose."

"Besides Rick."

Stone thought about it. "Okay, I'm stumped."

"Remember the man at Ralph Lauren in New York who looked like a comic book assassin?"

"Black clothes and hat, bald pate?"

"That's the one. When we walked home last night, he was on the other side of the boulevard, walking in the same direction."

"No. I'm sure I would have spotted him."

"He was wearing a tweed coat and a beret."

"Oops. Isn't it against the rules for an assassin to change costumes like that?"

"Are you kidding? What rules?"

"You mean there's no, well, code of honor?"

She poked him in the ribs. "No kidding."

"Then why didn't he take a shot at us?"

"At you."

"At me."

"Two reasons: One, he spotted one or more of our escorts. Or, two, he's one of ours instead of one of theirs."

"One of whose?"

"That remains to be seen."

"Why wouldn't you already know this sort of thing?"

"Perhaps you observed that, yesterday, we changed continents? Well, the cast changes, too, and changes are not always apparent."

"Maybe you should have a chat with Rick about that."

"I expect to. He'll be here in time for lunch, if I know Rick."

"I've already told Marie that we'll be three."

"We'd both better get some clothes on," she said.

The doorbell rang.

Rick gobbled up his pasta carbonara, then took a long swig of his wine. "I'm a happy man," he said, putting down his glass.

"I'm so glad," Stone replied. "I hope you're glad, too, about the level of my safety."

"Rocky said you refused to take all this seriously. Let me ask a question."

"Shoot."

"That's for assassins."

Stone groaned.

"My question is: Since your computer exploded in your office, why can't you get used to the idea that someone has dark plans for you?"

"Well, I look at it this way: the guy who screwed up my computer gave me a deadline of noon that day, and that's when it went off. I reckoned it was because I hadn't paid the extortion, not because he wanted to do me harm."

"Stone, when somebody plants an ounce of C-4 in a piece of electronic equipment that you use every day, he means you harm, or worse. Now, if we're going to keep you alive, you have to stop being so fucking naïve."

Stone sighed. "Oh, all right. I hereby place my person in the capable hands of you and Rocky, and I promise to do whatever you tell me."

"Don't leave the house," Rick said.

"I can't do that! I'm in Paris! Also, it would mean that the bad guy wins!"

"He's incorrigible," Rocky said to Rick. "We'll just have to cuff him to a radiator, or something."

"I can do that," Rick said, "after dessert."

After lunch, they went shopping, which meant that Stone stayed in the car with Rick, while Rocky ransacked the shops.

"I need to go to Charvet," Stone said. "I'm due for a fitting."

"I had a feeling that would come up," Rick said. "I've already assigned a team to Charvet, but you'll have to wait another hour

78

while they get into position."

"What will they look like, so I'll recognize them?"

"I'm not going to tell you, and don't try to figure it out. Just relax and get your suit fitted."

"Rick, I'm sorry. I know I'm infringing on your real work."

"My real work has been very boring for the past couple of weeks. So, believe it or not, you're a welcome change."

"Glad to be of help," Stone said.

They arrived at the great store on time, and Stone, looking neither to the left nor right, went directly to the elevator and up to the tailoring floor. His fitting awaited him. The tailor's fitting assistant looked a little beefy for his line of work, so Stone immediately assumed he was one of Rick's. When they were back in the car, Stone questioned him about it.

"Negative," Rick said, "but I know the one you're talking about. He plays Rugby every weekend."

"Then who . . . ?"

Rick put a finger to his lips. "Shhh."

Stone shut up.

79

12

When they arrived back at the gate to Stone's mews, he was surprised to see a man in a black raincoat and waterproof hat standing at the gate with a submachine gun, barely concealed.

"What the hell is that?" he demanded of Rick. "I thought we were being subtle."

"On reflection," Rick said, "I thought it might be better to advertise."

"Think of it as pest control," Rocky chimed in.

They got into the house without weapons being fired, and Stone invited Rick to stay for tea.

"That's veddy British of you," Rick said.

"I have that gene."

"I accept, if there are pastries involved."

"I assure you, there will be. Marie can't help herself."

They settled into the study, and Stone lit

a fire. It was the perfect accompaniment to the deluge outside.

"Okay, Rick," Stone said, "tell me what's really going on here."

Rick sighed. "Marie found four bugs in the house."

"Are we talking about pest control again?"

"We're talking about an electronics invasion," Rick replied.

"Who is doing this?"

"If we knew that, we would have already brought them into custody."

"Is it connected to the computer thing?"

"Yes, it is, and don't talk about it as if someone had stolen your laptop. The computer attack was a serious attempt on your life; the extortion thing was just window dressing. Of course, he may have been trying to make a buck, as well."

"I'm beginning to wish I hadn't asked," Stone said. "I liked being cavalier better."

"I know, buddy, but we can't tolerate this. Lance takes serious exception to this kind of activity, especially when it happens to somebody whose name is attached to his on a business card."

"What am I going to do, then?"

"Nothing, unless you want to go back to New York."

"When is this rain going to stop?"

81

"Around midnight, if my information is correct."

"Rocky, are you shopped out, yet?"

"I don't know. That's never happened before. What are the symptoms?"

"A sort of retail lassitude."

"Oh, so *that's* what it is. Maybe so."

"Okay, we'll go back to New York tomorrow morning, and you can rest up on the way for a fresh assault on the shops there."

"Will it be possible for me to go to my apartment for a couple of hours to create some rack space?"

"Do you need a carpenter for that?"

"No, just a few garbage bags."

"Sure, why not." Stone called Faith. "Wheels up at ten AM?"

"Sure. What do you want for lunch tomorrow?" Faith asked.

"Charcuterie, cheeses, and fresh bread?"

"Done."

Stone hung up. "Now, do we have to dine in, or is there someplace you feel comfortable taking us?"

"Tell you what, we have a protective operation going at Lasserre this evening. I could flesh out the detail to include you, I guess."

"Flesh away," Stone said. Lasserre was among his favorite restaurants in Paris. "But we'd like to feel that we're having a romantic dinner for two. Can you preserve that illusion?"

"I take it that excludes me from your table."

"Pretty much. I'm sure the Agency will still buy, if you have it in the kitchen."

"I'll be where you can't see me."

"I'll settle for that. Eight o'clock? And you can choose our table."

"Done."

"Rick," Rocky said.

"Yes?"

"Do you have an ID on our stalker from last night?"

"Oh, him. Russian, name of Izak Pentkovsky."

"Affiliation?"

"Ex-GRU, ex-KGB, now associated with a private group, one with bad intentions."

Stone groaned. "Not Russian Mob?"

"Maybe this week," Rick said.

"I thought you had killed all those guys!"

"A few of them, certainly not all."

"Is somebody holding a grudge?"

"Well, you're not their favorite guy," Rick replied. "Most of those we killed were because they were after you."

"I didn't see this in his file," Rocky said.

"Call it off the books, I guess. Stone

83

wasn't on the payroll at the time."

"Stone," she said, "are you on the Agency payroll now?"

"Not so's you'd notice," Stone replied. "I'm not turning in my law license just yet."

"That off-the-books stuff has a way of lingering with the Russians," Rocky said.

Rick shrugged. "They have long memories. You'd think their brains would be pickled in vodka by now, but noooo."

"Who's running things now?" Stone asked.

"The old guy, the one who hated you so much, died of a heart attack, probably brought on by the bullet in his brain."

"Who's the new guy?"

"Anton Pentkovsky," Rick replied. "Younger brother of your stalker, Izak."

"Nepotism in reverse?"

"Yeah. I didn't want to bring this up, but you did." Rick turned to Rocky. "Stone gets a little nervous when the Russian Mob comes up."

Stone held out a steady hand. "I'm not nervous."

"I wish you were," Rick said, "the situation would cost me less sleep."

"I don't see any bags under your eyes, Rick," Stone said.

"They're figurative, but they're there."

Rick tapped his temple with an index finger.

"How can we calm these people down, get them off my back?"

"Your head on a cocktail tray would do it, I think, but I take it that's off the table."

"Good guess. Anything less painful?"

"Rocky? Any ideas?"

"I could shoot Izak," she offered.

"As much fun as that would be, it would only make things worse."

"Define 'worse,' " Stone said.

"Dead sooner."

"Rocky," Stone said, "don't shoot Izak."

13

Lasserre occupied an entire townhouse on the Avenue Franklin Delano Roosevelt, and the dining room was upstairs from the reception area. The restaurant was a large, square room, with a grand piano in one corner, and — everyone's favorite feature — a large panel in the ceiling that slid silently open, to reveal a rose arbor on the roof and the night sky above it.

While they sipped a champagne *fraises des bois* (essentially a kir royale, but substituting a strawberry liqueur for the usual stuff — it cleared the palate and made the mouth ready for fine food), Stone had a look around the restaurant over his menu. Half the men were clad in fine European tailoring of one country or another, the others were in American suits of an expensive nature; the women were dressed to kill.

"See any assassins?" Rocky whispered from behind her menu.

"Not yet," Stone said. "Everyone seems too well-dressed for that kind of work."

"Yes, a meticulous workman doesn't want spatter on his Charvet suit, does he?"

Stone grimaced. "Let's change the subject to food." They did, and ordered directly.

To Stone's surprise, Rick La Rose appeared from the kitchen in a busboy's white jacket and began pouring ice water for the guests at their tables.

Rocky stifled a laugh. "I'll never let him live this down," she said.

"I think he's checking out décolletages, rather than assassins."

"You could be right."

"I usually am."

She arched an eyebrow at him.

"Not always, but usually."

Rocky sighed and ordered.

They had just finished their main courses and were watching the ceiling slide open when a small vase of flowers on their table exploded. There was no bang, just the tinkle of breaking china.

Rocky put a hand on Stone's arm. "Don't move. It's being taken care of. It's happening on the roof. I saw a barrel peeking out of the rose arbor." She looked at their butter dish, just behind the vase, and it had split in half. "The butter took a round," she said. "Same one as the vase."

Rick appeared at Stone's elbow and pretended to add water to his glass. "We've got to get you out of here," he said.

"Not until we've had dessert," Stone replied.

"Stone . . ."

"Whoever fired it missed, and your people have already roused him."

"You're not safe here."

"He could be waiting for us to hurry out the front door, couldn't he?"

"Possibly," Rick said through clenched teeth.

"Well, I'd rather be sitting where he's already missed, rather than encountering him outside. Let us know when the whole place is officially clear, but not before we've finished dessert."

Rick left the table with his pitcher of water.

"You've embarrassed him," Rocky said.

"*I'm* the one being shot at, and *he's* embarrassed?"

"Your logic is impeccable, I'll give you that. We're just as safe here as anywhere."

Dessert arrived, and Rick was right behind it, this time in a suit. "This way, please, sir, madame." He walked them to the elevator and got in with them. "The front door has been cleared, and so has the traffic," Rick said, fingering the little tear in the left shoulder of Stone's suit jacket. "We'll send this back to Charvet for repairs."

"Simpler to have it done in New York," Stone said.

Rick put them in the rear seat of the vehicle, then got into the front passenger seat. "We're going to take a circuitous route home, to give my people time to clear your house. How many shots did you hear?"

"None," Stone said, "but there must have been two. One couldn't have hit my shoulder and both dishes, the angle would have been wrong."

"I'll accept your judgment on that," Rick said. "The weapon was silenced. We found it on the roof."

"Anything interesting?"

"Russian light game rifle, folding stock, scope, short barrel. If he were a better shot, your head would have looked like the butter."

"What a nice thought!"

"We're moving up your flight time to six AM," Rick said.

"Swell."

"You can sleep on the airplane."

"I guess. I hope you got the check."

"We run an account there."

"Does the manager understand what happened?"

"I hope not. I'd hate for us to be banned."

"You'd better be back in their good graces before my next visit to Paris," Stone said. "Lasserre is one of my favorites."

They were back in Stone's New York house by early afternoon the next day. Stone's cell phone was ringing. "Yes, Lance?"

"Congratulations on your narrow escape from the Angel of Death," he said. "That's what the cognoscenti call Izak Pentkovsky."

"Nothing I did. The shooter was just unlucky."

"The Russians have probably already shot him by now; Lasserre is one of their ambassador's favorite restaurants."

"Well, we wouldn't want him to get a bad table," Stone said.

"There aren't any bad tables at Lasserre."

"I agree."

"I hope you also agree that this isn't over."

"I was afraid you'd say that," Stone replied. "Where would you like me to dine tonight?"

"At home."

"Agreed."

"I'll keep you posted on progress," Lance said, then hung up.

"Was that Lance?" Rocky asked.

"Who else?"

"What was his attitude?"

"Inscrutable. I'm not sure whether he was happy or sad that I survived."

"Stone, I'm sure he was happy. Why else would he have laid on all that security in Paris?"

"Of course, you're right. I guess I'm just tired of being a target."

"Are you tired of being so closely guarded?"

"Not by you, I'm not. Perhaps we should keep the level of my peril alive just enough to keep Lance interested in having you stay at my side."

"At some point, I'll be needed elsewhere," she said.

"Not by me," Stone replied.

14

Ed Rawls sat on the front porch of his house in Dark Harbor, Maine, on the island of Islesboro, in Penobscot Bay, munching scrambled eggs and sausages from the dish on the folding table at his elbow. There was a 12-gauge police riot shotgun lying across his lap; his only concession to gun safety was that there was not a round in the chamber.

His iPhone uttered a chirp that told him there was someone at his gate a hundred yards down his driveway. Ed picked up his iPhone and pressed an icon. A picture of two men in a car appeared on-screen, one of them at the wheel.

"Go away," Ed said into the phone.

"Mr. Rawls?"

"I'll tell you one more time before I set off the charge in the gatepost: Go away."

"I'm here at the behest of one far above us," the man said. "If you want to kill somebody, make it him."

"You're closer and easier," Rawls said.

"I'd like to speak to you on behalf of that person."

"Do it now, then."

"There are ears in the forest around here and on that Hinckley Picnic Boat about a hundred and fifty yards off your beach."

Rawls looked out at the water and squinted. Such a craft bobbed at anchor, and he could see someone moving in the cockpit. He pressed another icon on his iPhone, one controlling the gate. "One of you can walk up the driveway and live; more than one, and the other gets buckshot for breakfast."

"Understood," the man at the wheel said, and got out of the car.

Rawls pressed another icon and got a display of four images from cameras around the house. He watched as the man passed through the open gate, wearing khaki trousers, a lumberjack's shirt, and a barn coat. "Leave the gun on the gatepost," he said.

The man stopped, reached inside his coat, brought out a Colt .45 model 1911, and set it carefully on the gatepost.

"Proceed," Rawls said. "When you come around the corner of the house, you'd better have your hands in the air."

The man came around the corner of the house with his hands in the air. He didn't wait to be offered a seat but took the nearest porch chair.

"I didn't invite you to sit down," Rawls said.

"I don't really give a shit," the man said. "You going to shoot me for sitting down?"

"I could shoot you for the backup piece strapped to your left ankle," Rawls said. "Take it out and throw it at the driveway."

The man did so.

"All right, speak."

"Yesterday after the president's daily intelligence briefing, she asked a person to remain when the others left. She then inquired as to the safety measures taken to protect the life of her friend, Stone Barrington, upon whose life two attempts have been made, the most recent in Paris last night."

"Is he dead or alive?"

"Alive, so far."

"Who wants him dead?"

"From the available evidence, looks like the Russian Mob. The top guy is Pentkovsky, the younger. The elder brother appears to be on the case, as well."

"Those guys don't miss much. Why ain't Barrington dead?"

"Our people in Paris are good, too, and

94

one of ours is at Mr. Barrington's side at all times."

"She must be beautiful if Stone is sitting still for that."

"I'm told it is as you say."

"What do you want?"

The man looked around, as if there might be someone listening. "What I'm about to say is off the books and, in addition, was never said."

"Then why are you recording our conversation?" Rawls asked.

"I am not wearing a wire."

"Well, your man on the Hinckley has got a dish antenna the size of a pizza pointed at us. Don't that count?"

"All right, he's ours, and his companion has a sniper's rifle and a bead on your head, should your greeting get any less friendly. May we proceed?"

"All right, go ahead."

"Our very important person has been told by a very, very important person that the world would be a better place if the Pentkovskys were not in it, and has requested action to that effect. I stress that this is not an official request and is entirely off the books."

"So the president and Lance Cabot want me to off a Pentkovsky?"

"Two Pentkovskys — stressing that such a

thought never entered their heads nor passed their lips."

"And I'm supposed to do this for God, Country, and the American Way?"

"There is an aluminum camera case containing a million dollars in used, nonsequential fifty-, twenty-, and ten-dollar bills buried somewhere on this island. On corroboration of the successful completion of this task, the coordinates and a photograph of the site will be texted to you."

"You said two tasks."

The man gazed out to sea and thought about it for a moment. "All right, two million dollars. All of it will be in place before the next ferry leaves for the mainland."

"Whose money is it?"

"Yours, if you do the work; if not, nobody's. It will be returned to its usual resting place, to await another occasion when it is required. And you get the text only after both tasks are completed."

"What happens to it if I get killed? What about my heirs and assigns?"

"You have only one heir, and we couldn't care less about your assigns, if such exist."

Rawls thought about it for half a minute. "What is the geographical location of the persons named?"

"They'll both be in New York by dinner-time, and so will you, if you accept our offer and a ride. All your expenses will be covered, too, including transportation." He reached into his pocket and produced a thick envelope. "This contains fifty thousand dollars, to cover your costs, and we'll throw in a room at the Carlyle Hotel, already booked."

"I accept your offer and your money," Rawls said. "Toss over the envelope."

The man tossed the envelope and Rawls caught it with the reflexes of an old catcher, which he was. "All right," he said, "find your gun. It will take me a few minutes to pack some things and a couple of weapons."

"We have a rather special and versatile weapon in the car for you, along with a compact 9mm semiautomatic and silencer and leather for it, and ammo for each."

"You guys think of everything, don't you?" Rawls got up and went into the house. "I'll open the gate in fifteen minutes, and you can drive down here."

He went inside and closed the door.

97

15

Rawls got out of the car at the airstrip on Islesboro and watched a black helicopter appear on the horizon, as the two men unloaded his luggage. One of the men got back into the car and drove away.

"Where's he going?" Rawls asked his companion.

"To bury the rest of your fee; he'll get the ferry. We're going directly to MacArthur Airport, on Long Island, which is lightly used."

The helicopter landed with a surprising lack of noise; somebody in a nearby house wouldn't have heard it. A crew got out and dealt with Rawls's luggage, and he and the CIA officer got into the helicopter and put on headsets. The officer flipped a switch on the panel into which the headsets were plugged.

"Now we're on intercom, just the two of us," he said. "The pilot and copilot cannot

98

hear us, and we are not transmitting."

"Gotcha," Rawls said.

"My name is Jim, for these purposes, and you will communicate with me over this phone." He handed Rawls a white iPhone and gave him the four-digit access code. "The only number you can phone is mine, and you will receive all instructions from me and report all your actions on this phone alone. Clear?"

"As gin," Rawls replied.

Jim handed him a black file folder. "Everything you need in the way of background is in here. If there's anything else you need to know, ask me. If I don't know, I'll find out."

Rawls nodded.

"You will note from the file that the Pentkovskys are also staying at the Carlyle, one floor below you. They are having dinner this evening at Caravaggio, a fancy Italian restaurant around the corner from the Carlyle. It would be a good place to have a drink at the bar and get a good look at them. You are not to kill them there or at the Carlyle or on a New York City street, except after dark, do you understand?"

"What's left?" Rawls asked.

"You may kill them in a vehicle on the street at any time. If you are seriously wounded or at risk of being taken by the

99

authorities, you must not be taken alive. Is this clearly understood?"

Rawls looked thoughtful but said nothing. *"Do you understand?"*

"I guess if that happened, life wouldn't be worth living anyway, so yes,"

"Good decision."

Rawls knew that if he had not satisfactorily answered that question, he would have departed the helicopter well ahead of its arrival at MacArthur Field, probably over Long Island Sound, where an outgoing tide would soon introduce his carcass to the Atlantic Ocean.

"Do they travel in an armored vehicle?"

"Perhaps, but the weapon I have given you will penetrate the windows. Fire once for penetration, then again, through that hole for the kill. I need hardly tell you that we would find it preferable for you to kill them both at once; otherwise, we'd just have the other one walking around, raising the alarm with his people."

"How much security do they travel with?"

"Normally a driver and another man riding shotgun, and two men in a following car. You may kill whoever you have to in order to get a clear shot at them or to avoid being shot yourself. You are not to carry any form of personal identification while working — not even a credit card — but you may carry all the cash you require for walking-around money. If you become a fatality, your room at the Carlyle will be deep-cleaned, and any personal effects, except for clothing, will be removed and sent to your daughter at an appropriate moment. Your body will be cremated by a reputable Manhattan undertaker, and your ashes offered to your daughter. If she declines them, they'll do God knows what with them."

"I want my daughter to have the money."

"She will have it, if you complete your task before dying. We do not pay for work undone."

None of this came as a surprise to Rawls, who had given similar briefings to others over the years.

"What is my daughter's address?" Rawls asked.

"It is 1010 Fifth Avenue," Jim replied, "across from the Metropolitan Museum, apartment 41A." He gave Rawls a card with her phone number and his own.

The copter rose and flew quietly on toward Long Island at three thousand feet, in clouds. Rawls could catch an occasional glimpse of the ground. After nearly two hours of flight — helicopters are not all that fast — the aircraft slowed and descended, apparently on an instrument approach. As they set down, an SUV pulled up outside, and his luggage was loaded.

"Good luck," Jim said. He didn't offer his hand.

Rawls checked into his room, which was large and comfortable, and switched on the TV for background noise while he unpacked.

He found some little bottles of whiskey in the bar fridge and poured himself a bourbon, then he sat down and sort of watched CNN. He reflected that, when he got up this morning, he would not have guessed he'd be sleeping at the Carlyle that night. He found a menu and ordered a club sandwich from room service.

16

Rocky sat up in bed; it was late afternoon. "What are we doing for dinner?"

"We're going out," Stone said firmly. "I'm tired of ducking these people. If they try to shoot us, we'll shoot back. I know that's contrary to your instructions, but there is such a thing as cabin fever."

"Am I part of that?"

"Negative. I'd have run amok days ago, if I hadn't had you for company."

"And sex."

"Oh, yes," he said, kissing her. "What kind of food do you want?"

"Not French," she said. "Italian, but elegant Italian."

"That can be arranged," he said, picking up a phone and booking them into a restaurant.

They arrived at the restaurant on time and were greeted by Gianni, a former headwaiter

103

at Elaine's, and seated promptly at a table with a good view of the whole room.

"Well chosen," Rocky said. "Lance would approve."

"If I know Lance, he's watching us on his iPhone right now."

"I wouldn't be surprised." They were halfway through their first drinks and had ordered, when Stone froze, his gaze fixed on the front door.

"What's wrong?" Rocky asked.

"Don't look now, as the saying goes, but soon. I think one of the two men who entered is the supposed assassin we saw in New York and Paris."

Rocky took a sip of her drink, laughed, and checked out the new customers being seated. "You are correct," she said, nuzzling his shoulder, "that is Izak Pentkovsy, and the man with him is his younger brother. We have somehow landed in the hornet's nest. Did you do this intentionally, in a fit of misplaced bravado?"

"I did not. I'm not that brave."

"I don't see any bulges under jackets, so they're probably not armed."

"The Italian tailors they have apparently been visiting are skilled at hiding bulges."

"I'll keep an eye on them," she said.

"Rocky," Stone said, "do you remember a

story from the Agency, now a legend, about how Katharine Lee, during her tenure there, was able to nail an Agency officer who had been blackmailed into supplying secrets to the Soviets, and who Kate exposed? He later went to prison for a couple of years, until he was pardoned by Will Lee, after he became president."

"I do remember that. What was his name?"

"His name was Ed Rawls, and he just came into the restaurant and took a seat at the bar."

Rawls took note of him, and Stone raised a single finger from the table and got a tiny nod in response.

"I've stumbled into a few coincidences in my career," Rocky said, "but never anything like this. I have a feeling that one corner of this triangle has been set up, but I don't know which one it is."

"Excuse me for a moment," Stone said. He rose and walked to the men's room. He had been there for about a minute, washing his hands, when Ed Rawls entered the room, locked the door behind him, and checked the stalls.

"What the fuck are you doing here?" Rawls asked, mildly.

"I might ask the same question of you," Stone replied.

"Working."

"Really? I'm playing. What kind of work are you doing?"

"Surveillance, at the moment."

"Me?"

"No, stupid, two Russian gentlemen."

"Oh, them."

"You know them?"

"Only by reputation."

"They're dying to know you."

"I've heard something about that."

"One of us should leave immediately," Rawls said.

"That would be you," Stone replied. "We've just ordered the risotto. It takes time, and we're hungry."

"I'll communicate later," Rawls said. He unlocked the door and left the room.

Stone dried his hands, flushed a urinal for effect, and went back to his table.

"What was that?" Rocky said. "He followed you into the men's room."

"I noticed that," Stone replied. "But now he's gone." He nodded toward the bar, where Rawls's stool had been vacated.

"Well, thank God for that. Do you think Lance sent him?"

"No, I don't. I think if Lance knew about it he would be extremely upset."

"Why?"

"Because Ed Rawls is still persona non grata with a certain strata of people at Langley, and Lance is probably among them."

"What do you think is happening?"

"Rawls is the kind of ex-officer that someone might tap for a little off-the-books work. Lance would never get near anything like that. He'd be afraid he'd end up testifying about it before the Senate Intelligence Committee."

"And that's the last place on earth Lance would want to be."

"Tell me," Stone said, "did you mention to any of your people where we were having dinner tonight?"

"No, not a one. I wanted us to have some privacy."

"Well, this is the very antithesis of privacy."

"It certainly is. Do you think Rawls was following us?"

"No, in the men's room, he mentioned a connection with two Russians. It's them, not us. Ed was upset that we were here."

"Do you think the Pentkovskys made him?"

"No. They might have if he'd stayed for dinner and left after they did, but Ed would be too subtle for a boneheaded play like

107

that. Whatever you may think of him, he's a fine operator."

"Do you think we should leave?"

"No, they saw Ed come into the men's room and saw him leave. I don't think they've even noticed us. Let's not look at them again."

Their risotto *fruiti di mare* arrived, and they ate it with gusto and a bottle of Puligny-Montrachet. After that, they had Italian cheesecake for dessert, then espresso and cognac.

While they were on coffee, the Pentkovskys got up and left.

"Whew!" Rocky said. "I thought they'd never go."

"Everybody goes, eventually," Stone mused. "Do you hear any gunfire from outside?"

"No, why do you ask?"

"Because it occurs to me that Ed Rawls might have been hired to kill them, not just follow them."

"You really think that?"

"Tell me, Rocky, would the Agency you know and love stoop to that sort of action to protect you and me?"

Rocky thought about that. "You, maybe. Not me."

"I'm flattered," Stone said.

"Careful," she replied, "flattery can get you dead."

"Careful," she replied. "Hattie can get you dead."

17

Rawls stood in a darkened doorway on Madison Avenue and waited. He had done hundreds of stakeouts in his time, and the waiting didn't bother him. His back did, though, and he leaned against the masonry wall behind him and pressed his spine straight. As long as he held that position, he had no pain.

Madison Avenue was quiet enough at this hour that he heard their footsteps as they turned the corner. He retrieved the 9mm silenced pistol and watched them head uptown on the other side of the street. His sight line kept being interrupted as they passed trees and signage. He got a clear shot at one now and then, but not both of them, and he didn't want to take the risk of being spotted if he followed them too closely uptown. They had seen him at the bar, and the last thing he needed right now was to become a familiar face to them.

They crossed with the light at Seventy-sixth Street, then were out of sight when he emerged from the doorway. Short of sprinting up the street, causing him to be noticed by passersby, he had no way of catching up before they turned into the Carlyle's side entrance.

He walked slowly up Madison to give them time to clear the lobby, then turned into the main entrance, where the entrances were to the Café Carlyle, a nightclub, and Bemelmans Bar, a saloon with music. He looked through the glass doorway of Bemelmans, past the pianist, and saw the Pentkovskys sitting at the bar. He quickly side-stepped the door and went up to his room. No use taking the chance of being sighted by them again.

He sat down on the bed, fished out the iPhone he had been given, and dialed the only number he had.

"This is Jim."

"This is who you figure it is," Rawls said.

"Do you have sight of them?"

"I did, in the restaurant. But they left, and I couldn't get a clean shot."

"What is a clean shot?"

"Let me put it this way: You've given me a silenced weapon. Do you want to hear the sound of shattering shop windows on Madi-

111

son Avenue?"

"Certainly not."

"Neither do I. That's what I mean by a clean shot, that and no obstacles. My question is: Do you have any details of their movements tomorrow?"

"I'll check my sources and call you back." He hung up.

Rawls got undressed for bed, and he was brushing his teeth when the phone rang. He rinsed, spat, then picked it up. "Yeah?"

"They've got a breakfast meeting at eight AM tomorrow at the Drake Hotel restaurant," Jim said.

"That will be jammed with people and employees. It's the hottest breakfast spot on the Upper East Side, and there's no good way out at that time of day."

"I'll take that as a no," Jim said.

"Good guess. What else?"

"They're having dinner at the University Club."

"Forget it. Do they ever go below Forty-second Street?"

"Little Italy sometimes."

"That could work very nicely," Rawls said. "As you may recall, removals have been performed there before. The neighborhood even made it into *The Godfather.* I'll need to know where they're going and at what

112

time, and anything else you can provide."

"I'll work on it," Jim said, then hung up.

"Let me get this straight," Lance Cabot said. "You, the Pentkovskys, and Ed Rawls were all in the same restaurant at the same time last night?"

"Improbable, isn't it?"

"Improbable on purpose," Lance said.

"Who would have a motive to get us all there at the same time?"

"I don't know. That's what's annoying me. I mean, I can see how you and the Pentkovskys might coincidentally book into the same restaurant. I just can't figure why Ed would be there."

"Lance," Stone said, "this sounds to me like inner workings of the Agency, and that is something I can't help you with."

"You can, if I say you can," Lance said, stubbornly.

"Okay, how can I help?"

Lance thought about it. "You can't," he said, then hung up.

Stone looked across the bed at Rocky, who was demolishing a breakfast sausage. "Lance is angry," he said.

"He only gets angry when he's made a mistake, or someone else has and won't admit it."

113

"Has Lance ever admitted a mistake?"

"Not in this millennium," she replied. "He's famous in the Agency for not doing that."

"Neither he nor I can figure Ed Rawls's being at Caravaggio last evening, along with the Pentkovskys."

"Do you know what kind of work Rawls specialized in during his career at the Agency?"

"I didn't know agents specialized."

"Of course they do, dummy. Think about it."

"I've thought about it, and you're right."

"Good answer."

"I have the impression that Ed was a master of all trades while he was serving."

"Then he would be a very valuable agent, indeed. Did he ever, to your knowledge, do wet work?"

"Like scuba diving?"

Rocky sighed. "Work that would be illegal if it weren't being done by an agent. Maybe even then."

"My guess, from former conversations, would be yes. He's hinted as much."

"And he's fully retired now? On pension?"

"I believe so."

"Is he the sort of guy who . . . if the Agency asked him to . . . well . . . get his

114

feet wet, he would do it?"

"Again I'm guessing, but probably."

"Do you think he might have been at the restaurant last night in pursuit of such work?"

"Maybe," Stone muttered.

"Somebody in the restaurant?"

"I think so. During our encounter in the men's room he seemed angry at me for being there."

"Did you recognize anybody in the restaurant except Rawls and the Pentkovskys?"

"One mafioso, who seems always to be there."

"Not him."

"Then it has to be either the Pentkovskys or . . ."

"Finish that sentence."

"You."

"No, no, no, no, no," Stone sputtered.

"You were both present."

"You were present, too," Stone pointed out.

"If they wanted to get rid of me, they'd just ship me off to some Central American post with no air-conditioning and lots of reptiles, two things that I can't stand. They're in my file."

"I'd love to read your file."

"Don't you dare!"

18

Rawls was awakened by heavenly harp music at what seemed to be an unseemly hour. He sat up in bed, seeking the source. His attention was directed to the bedside table, where his two iPhones were charging. One of them was emitting that music, until he managed to shut it off. Eight o'clock, the bedside instrument said.

Shortly, the same phone rang. "Yes?"

"It's Jim."

"Swell. Make a note: I rise at ten."

"Okay," Jim said. "Our friends are lunching at a Chinese restaurant called Hong Fat, at twelve-thirty."

"Address?"

"Chinatown." Jim hung up.

Rawls ordered breakfast, got into a shower, and was clean again by the time the waiter rolled in the cart. After breakfast he checked the weather on his iPhone: raining a lot until after 6 PM. He googled the address for Hong Fat.

At eleven o'clock, Rawls dressed, armed himself, and got into his trench coat and a hat. He didn't take the hotel's umbrella, because it was emblazoned with its name. He went downstairs and asked the doorman to get him a cab, and as he waited, a man came by selling umbrellas and plastic raincoats. He bought one of each.

It took, as he had imagined, nearly an hour to get down to Chinatown, what with traffic and the rain. He got out a block away from the restaurant, put on the raincoat, opened the umbrella, and walked up one side of the street and back. Hong Fat was plainly decorated, without dragon screens or potted plants. It seated few, and practically every seat could be viewed from outside. He crossed the street and walked down the block again, stopping under an awning across the street from the restaurant. His plan was simple: wait for them to study the menu, when they wouldn't be looking for trouble.

They were ten minutes late and were shown to a table near the door. Rawls checked for their security while he waited for them to get out of their raincoats and sit down. He saw none. As soon as they were absorbed with the menus, he moved the

117

pistol to a trench coat pocket, crossed the street, furled his umbrella, left it in the doorway, and opened the door. He stepped inside, took the pistol from his pocket, shot each of them once in the head, then turned around, exited the restaurant, picked up the umbrella, and walked around the corner, where he lost the plastic raincoat but kept the umbrella, then continued on his way.

He got lucky with a cab: two people got out of one, and he claimed it, asking the driver to take him to Bloomingdale's. As they neared the department store, fifty minutes later, he called the number.

"This is Jim."

"The work is done," he said. "E-mail me the directions to the honeypot."

"Not quite," Jim said.

"Say again?"

"One of them is still alive."

Rawls was stunned. "Which one?"

"The elder brother, Izak. He's at Bellevue Hospital under his own name. The place is crawling with media, print and TV. The other one is in the city morgue by now. What went wrong?"

"Nothing. One each, under the hair."

"Call me when *all* the work is done." He hung up.

"Driver, let's go to Bellevue Hospital."

"Anything wrong?"

"My wife called. Her ulcer is acting up."

Three quarters of an hour later, Rawls got of the cab at the nearest corner, walked to the emergency entrance, and strolled past. There were three TV trucks outside. A half dozen cops were patrolling the sidewalk, more inside.

He got another cab from an arriving driver. "Seventy-fifth and Madison," he said, sitting back in the seat. He should have shot them both twice in the head, he knew, but he had been afraid that somebody, like a civilian, might have tried to jump him before he could get all the rounds off.

Shit!

The cab made its way up Madison, and Rawls was eventually back at the Carlyle. He hung up his coat and hat to dry, made a cradle of pillows on the bed, and turned on a local news channel, famous for covering events that had just happened. They even had a copy of Izak's head X-ray, which showed a nick in the occipital skull, made by his bullet, which appeared not to have entered the brain, just ricocheted off the bone. It would have bled a lot and the shock would probably have rendered him unconscious, causing him to collapse like a mortally wounded man.

Amateur hour, he thought. He must really be getting old. He didn't want to wait for Izak to get discharged from Bellevue, but neither did he relish the idea of prowling the halls, looking for an opportunity to kill the man, without getting shot by the cops or Pentkovsky's security.

It was clear that he had to revisit the hospital, but not until tomorrow, when things had calmed down and someone might get careless.

The following morning Stone finished the first section of the *Times* and tossed it to Rocky when she came out of the shower. "Now we know what Ed Rawls was doing at Caravaggio," he said, "and where he was at lunchtime yesterday. He must be kicking himself."

Rocky read all of the piece, which featured Izak's X-ray. "How old is Rawls? I mean, he missed one at what, twelve feet?"

"A little too old, apparently, but he's also relentless, and he won't let this go until he's finished the job. Whoever hired him must be withholding payment until both brothers are dead."

Stone's cell phone rang. "Yes, Lance?"

"Now we know what Rawls was doing at

Caravaggio, eh?"

"Funny you should mention that."

"Yes, I know, you thought of it first."

"As soon as I saw the *Times*," Stone said.

"Ed is not going to stop, you know."

"I know. At least he's not after me."

"There's something to be said for that," Lance said. "You should stay out of anyplace Rawls might go."

"How the hell would I know where he might go?"

"Well, anyplace you've taken him in the past."

"There are probably a dozen such places. What do I have to do? Stay home until the Russians find Ed and deal with him?"

"Well, don't try to help him. That's a quick way to stop a bullet."

"I've no intention of helping him," Stone said.

"I know very well that you have a soft spot for Ed," Lance said. "You've helped each other before."

"I don't think he'll ask," Stone said.

"You go right on believing that," Lance replied.

"Bye, Lance." Stone hung up.

"I take it that was Lance," Rocky said.

"Good guess."

"Does he think you're helping Rawls?"

"He's afraid I might try to," Stone said. His secure cell phone rang again. "What now, Lance?" he asked.

"It's not Lance," Rawls said.

19

Stone recovered enough to say, "How are you?"

"Come have a seat in your garden, and I'll explain it to you."

Stone recalled that Ed had stayed with him a couple of times in the past, and that he had given him a key. "Ten minutes," he said and hung up.

" 'Ten minutes'?" Rocky asked. "Was that intended for me or your caller?"

"My caller," Stone said, pulling on his pants and a Polo shirt. "I've got to go speak with him."

"It's Rawls, isn't it?"

"This is a bad time to be as smart as you're supposed to be," Stone said. "I'll be back."

"I'll be here," she said, slithering under the covers.

Stone went downstairs, through the kitchen, and out into the garden, where Ed

Rawls was sitting at a table under an umbrella, sipping from a glass of lemonade. Helene, the cook, had always liked him.

Stone sat down, and immediately Helene brought him a glass of lemonade. He took a big swallow. "Well," he said. "I thought you might be dead by now."

"Same here," Rawls drawled.

"You or me?"

"Either or both."

"In that case, nice of you to lead them here."

"I didn't lead anybody. I haven't used the garden entrance for more than a year, and I don't allow myself to be followed from crime scenes."

"You're slipping, Ed," Stone said. "If the *New York Times* got the scene right."

"The guy dipped his head to sip his tea as I was squeezing off the second round," Rawls said. "Could have happened to anybody, and I didn't have time for two apiece."

"I'm surprised you haven't visited him in Bellevue yet."

"Oh, I have, at least as close as it was possible to get. There are two complete sets of men with guns watching over him."

"How many of them are looking for you?"

"None. I have no connection with the crime scene."

124

"You have a connection with Izak at Caravaggio, remember? He would have seen you go into the men's room after me."

"I left immediately after that; he never set eyes on me again."

"Or if he did, his memory might be affected by the bullet to the back of the head."

"He never made me."

"So why are you still here? I should think you'd be back in Dark Harbor by now."

"So would I, but I don't get the hidden location of my fee until the work is completed."

"I hope you aren't here to ask me to help," Stone said.

"Of course not. I'm here to tell you that whoever is replacing the younger Pentkovsky will be looking for you."

"Why would I interest him?"

"Because they don't know about me, so instead of looking for a needle in a haystack, they'll be using a scythe to clear the field of candidates for Anton's murder. You are the most recent guy the Pentkovskys wanted dead."

It annoyed Stone that he hadn't thought of that himself. "Do you have a suggestion, Ed?"

"I have two: One, don't get dead. Two, don't get *me* dead."

"Are our fates somehow entwined?"

"I should have thought that was obvious."

"Not to me."

"Well, the GRU's files are very likely just as good as the Agency's. And anybody reading either of ours will find out a lot about the other, most of which will be interesting to them."

That was a disquieting thought. "How can I help, Ed?"

"I need shelter."

"Now?"

"Almost. Right after I clear out of my room at the Carlyle."

"All right. Use the key you've got to enter my basement through a door on Third Avenue, marked 'Private.' A tunnel will take you to my garage, then walk up one flight, take a left and enter the house next door to mine. There's a ground-floor bedroom, overlooking the garden. Dig in there. Helene will see you don't starve or thirst. If you need to contact me, use your Agency cell, but call me on my civilian iPhone. I don't want Lance or anybody else there to see a record of conversations between us on those phones."

"That sounds perfect."

"Follow me." Stone led him into the house and into the garage, then to the room next door. "One other thing," Stone said. "I know you're not going to stop, but I don't want to know where, when, or how you collect your money."

"That goes without saying," Rawls replied.

"Where were the Pentkovskys staying?"

"At the Carlyle, one floor below me."

"I suggest you don't go back for your clothes; their people will be all over the hotel. Call the front desk and tell them you've had to take an emergency flight out, so they should pack your bags and leave them in their garage. I'll send my man, who is very careful, to fetch them and bring them here."

"That's very good, Stone. You'd have made a good field agent."

"Tell me that when I've lived another week," Stone replied. Then he left Rawls to his privacy.

Stone went back to his room and found Rocky just where he had left her. He began stripping down.

"You've seen Ed Rawls, haven't you?" she asked.

"I don't want to hear about Rawls anymore," he replied. "I have other things on my mind that are more important. For one, I am now genuinely concerned for my safety

127

and yours." He got into bed and reached for her.

"Nobody will ever find us here," Rocky said, "unless they hear your pitiful cries."

Later, Stone explained Fred's mission to him. "The bags are brown alligator and have tags that say CREW."

"Question," Fred said. "Do they know he's leaving the hotel?"

"As far as I know, they don't know he's staying there."

"Mr. Barrington," Fred said, "do you mind if I change the license plates on the Bentley?"

"You have other license plates?" Stone asked.

"Some that I bought at a roadside shop in Florida last year."

"Good idea," Stone said. "But don't get stopped by the police, and if you do, call me at once."

"Yes, sir."

Fred changed the New York plates for Florida ones, made of plastic, but credible.

He drove uptown to the Carlyle, pulled into the garage, and immediately spotted Rawls's luggage, piled near a soft drink machine.

"May I help you, sir?" a uniformed at-

128

tendant said.

"I'm here for those," Fred replied, pointing and simultaneously pressing the switch that opened the trunk. The attendant loaded them into the car and closed the trunk door. Fred gave him a fifty. "If anybody asks, the cases were never here," he said, then backed out and drove away.

Ed Rawls went next door and looked for Stone's secretary, Joan Robertson.

"Hi, Ed, I hear you're with us next door for a bit," Joan said.

"I am, Joan. Tell me, I'd like to make myself an ID badge, and I need a computer with photoshopping software, a color printer, some photographic-finish paper, and a laminating machine."

"Come with me," she said, leading him through Stone's office and into a supply room with a small desk. "Here you are," she said, "the paper's on the shelf, there, the software is on the computer, and the laminating machine is over there," she said, "next to the paper cutter."

"Thank you, ma'am," Ed said. "I owe you two dozen roses."

"I'll hold you to that," Joan said. "Anything else? Stone told me to shop for you. He doesn't want you coming and going."

"Do you know where to find a medical supply store — you know, where you buy crutches and wheelchairs and bedpans and the sort?"

"I do."

"Could you pick me up a surgical cap, a lab coat, some latex gloves, a packet of surgical masks, a stethoscope, and one of those little medical valises?"

"Sure. If you need somebody to operate on, I'll volunteer."

"I wouldn't impose," Ed said. "Oh, and get me one of those lanyard things with a clip at the bottom to hold a badge." She left, and Rawls sat down at the computer and googled Bellevue Hospital. He scrolled through various pages until he found a page of photographs of medical staff. He found one of a man who slightly resembled him, but with more hair, wearing scrubs. He took a photo of himself standing before a white wall, then enlarged the man's ID badge and photoshopped his face onto it, then he changed the man's name to Gregory Mffisiane, M.D., shrank the card to ID size, and printed a half dozen of them. He selected one, trimmed it, and ran it through the laminating process, then trimmed the corners. "Good morning, Dr. Mffisiane," he said to the badge. "I'll bet people have

131

trouble remembering your name." He also invented a prescription form with his new name on it and printed a few of those, then taped the edges to make a pad.

An hour or so later, Joan returned with the things he'd asked for, and he reimbursed her, over her protests.

Rawls waited until later that afternoon so he could arrive at the hospital during a shift change, then he found the doctors' locker room and an empty locker. He left his coat inside and put on the lab coat and the cap, to cover his thinning hairline. He hung the stethoscope and the ID around his neck, and walked out into the hallway. He strode purposefully down the hallway until he found an unmanned nurse's station, checked the patients' list, and found Pentkovsky, I., a few doors down the hall. He looked that way, and saw a uniformed cop sitting on a folding chair outside the room, reading the *New York Post*. Rawls walked past the room until he saw a sign for the pharmacy and went inside.

A nurse was giving instructions to her shift replacement, a very young nurse, and Rawls waited patiently until the older woman had left. "Good afternoon," he said to the other nurse.

132

"Good afternoon," she replied. "What can I do for you, Doctor?"

Rawls whipped out the prescription pad he had made and wrote something on it. "I need 50 cc's of morphine and a large syringe. I'm recharging a patient's automated doser. This will do him until this time tomorrow."

The nurse glanced at the prescription, then took a bunch of keys from her pocket and unlocked a drawer. She set the vial on the counter, then got a syringe from another drawer. "There you are," she said.

Rawls thanked her, then put the items in his lab coat pocket and left the pharmacy. He walked back to where the cop sat and held up his ID. "I'm checking the patient's vital signs," he said.

"A nurse did that a few minutes ago," the cop replied.

"Then I'm checking up on the nurse," Rawls replied with a grin.

The cop leaned over and examined Rawls's badge. "Okay, Dr. Mimm . . ." He didn't make it through the name.

"Just call me Dr. Greg. Everybody does."

"Go on in."

Rawls entered the room and found Pentkovsky, mouth open, staring at the ceiling. They had him on painkillers, Rawls thought, and that was fine with him. He broke the cap on the morphine bottle, filled the syringe, and injected the clear fluid into the man's IV fluids bag, then repeated until the bottle was empty. That would take a while to drip in and do its work. He returned the empty bottle and syringe to his pocket and left the room.

He went back to the doctors' locker room, packed his things into the small valise, put on his coat, and walked down the hallway to the exit at the opposite end of the corridor. Moments later, he was in a cab. "Bloomingdale's," he said to the driver.

Outside the department store he tossed the valise into a dumpster at a construction site across the street, along with the morphine bottle and the empty syringe. He walked across Third Avenue and through the store to Lexington and found another taxi there. He got out a block short and walked the rest of the way, crossing the street, doubling back and checking for tails. Finally, he let himself through the door marked PRIVATE, and made his way to his room.

That evening, an alarm went off at a nurse's station at Bellevue: a cardiac arrest down the hall. She picked up a phone. "Code Blue in 127. Repeat, Code Blue in 127," then she ran down the hall.

The following morning, Rawls checked the hourly news and saw the report of Pentkovsky's death, of cardiac arrest at Bellevue. The tox screen would take a few days, he knew.

He picked up his second cell phone and called the number.

"This is Jim."

"This is the other guy who has this number. The project is completed."

"Yeah, I heard it on the news. What means?"

"Overdose of morphine, but they won't know that for a few days. It's pretty busy around there."

"Okay, I'll e-mail you instructions and photos of the area. You won't have any trouble finding it."

"If I don't find it, Jim, I'll find you," Rawls said. "And if I so much as see another man anywhere near the site, I'll kill him."

"No problem," Jim said. "It's all there, in two small suitcases, about three feet underground. Take a shovel."

"Right."

"You want the chopper back to the island?"

Rawls thought about that. "No, I'll make my own way," he said. Nobody was going to kick him out of a helicopter into Penobscot Bay.

21

Rawls had dinner in his room and slept like a baby. The following morning, he called an air charter service he knew in Caldwell, New Jersey, west of Teterboro. He hired a Cessna 182 for a trip to Bangor, Maine, wheels up the next day at ten AM.

At seven the next morning he packed, and Fred insisted on driving him to Caldwell. The aircraft was waiting on the ramp, and a man in a leather jacket was leaning on the door. "I'm the charterer," Ed said to him; "are you my ride?"

"I am for six hundred bucks," the man said.

Rawls handed him the money and, while the man counted it, stowed his luggage in the rear compartment, then got into the right front seat. He fastened his seat belt, opened the *New York Times* that Fred had given him, then put on the available headset and unplugged it. He didn't want any conversation.

The pilot took the hint, started the airplane, ran through a checklist via his own headset and got a clearance. He took off and, at the direction of air traffic control, climbed to eight thousand feet.

Rawls read through the paper, checking the GPS now and then. When they were halfway there, Rawls plugged in his headset. "You read me?"

"I read."

"I have a change of destination: cancel IFR and descend to three thousand feet. Identifier is 57 Bravo." Rawls entered the identifier himself into the GPS, then pressed DIRECT and turned on the autopilot. He spun in the new altitude. The airplane swung to the right and descended.

"How much runway there?" the pilot asked.

"Two thousand four hundred fifty feet," Rawls replied. "You won't need it all, and we're cutting off half an hour from the trip, so don't ask for more money."

"It's your charter," the man said.

Rawls unplugged his headset and returned to his paper. Ten minutes before their ETA he put down the paper, plugged in the headset, and pointed straight ahead.

"Twelve o'clock and eight miles."

"Got it. Wind sock says land to the north."

They touched down and pulled over to the ramp. "No need to shut down," Rawls said. "I'll get my bags." He got out, emptied the luggage compartment, walked out of the way, and gave the pilot a thumbs-up. A minute later, Rawls was calling for a cab, and the airplane was climbing away to the south.

At home, Rawls tossed his bags onto the bed, got his shotgun and a shovel, and got into his Jeep. He tapped the coordinates into his iPhone and followed directions back toward the airport, then turned north on a quiet lane. He stopped and checked the photographs he had been sent. Turn right at an old mailbox that had had a baseball bat taken to it by a teenager years before. Twenty yards later, he spotted his marker: a stake driven into the ground, with six inches showing. He pulled over to the side of the road and got out with the shotgun. He checked out the area; nothing but trees in sight. He loosened the stake with his shovel, then pulled it out of the earth and started digging. Three feet down he made contact with something. He got a trowel from the Jeep, knelt down, and did the rest of his digging slowly and carefully. Finally, he had exposed an old Samsonite suitcase, and he worked around it, looking for wires or other signs of booby trapping. Finally, he got a length of rope from the Jeep, tied one end to the suitcase handle and the other to the vehicle. He backed up slowly, then, as the rope tautened, even more slowly. The case came free. He dragged it a few feet and stopped.

He turned on a small, powerful flashlight and went over the case again; looked okay. He opened the two latches slowly, then tipped open the case with his shovel, exposing two FedEx envelopes, each with something bulky inside. He closed the case, put it in the back of the Jeep, and drove home.

There, he scissored open both envelopes and found amounts of cash inside each. He counted the bundles and came up with a million dollars. Jim was short.

Rawls took out the second iPhone and called the number. "This is Jim."

"Not for long. You're short."

"Hey, can't you take a joke? My guy didn't have time to make the second delivery before the ferry left. He's on the water now, and he'll drop the second case on your dock."

"No, he won't. He'll walk up the dock to the house and set it on the front porch. Then he'll open the case and dump out the contents. If he does anything else, I'll kill him where he stands. Is that all perfectly clear?"

"Yes."

"And you tell him I have no sense of humor at all."

"I'll pass that on. Give him an hour. It'll be dark when he gets there. He'll flash a light at you three times. You flash back twice." Jim hung up.

Rawls walked back inside, went to the bedroom, opened one of his bags, and removed the special weapon Jim had given him. He inspected it, snapped in a fresh magazine. Then he went to the kitchen, made a cup of coffee, put the kitchen scissors in his pocket, and went out to the porch. He sat down in a comfortable wicker chair, laid the rifle across his lap, and sipped his coffee, waiting for it to get dark.

Rawls was tired, and he dozed now and then. It had just gotten dark when he heard the sound of an idling engine coming out of the dark. He got up, worked the rifle's action, and stood behind a post on the porch, resting the rifle barrel on a protruding nail.

141

He flipped the scope to the night setting and sighted down the barrel. He flinched when the spotlight flashed three times; it took him a moment to recover his vision in that eye. He flashed twice with his flashlight. The boat continued in.

It bumped against the dock's rubber padding and a man got out and took a single line to a cleat, then somebody aboard handed him a suitcase. Rawls sighted onto his chest. "Come ahead!" he shouted.

The man walked slowly up the dock, came ashore, and walked toward the house.

"Right up the steps," Rawls said, and the man climbed the steps. Rawls turned, keeping the barrel pointing toward the man, and the post between himself and the idling boat. The man was wearing a lumberjack's shirt and a mask made of a bandanna. "Open the case and shake out the contents onto the porch," Rawls said.

The man followed the instructions.

Rawls tossed the kitchen scissors into the case. "Cut both envelopes open and empty them into the case."

The man did so. Piles of money lay there.

"You can go now. Don't run, or I'll shoot you in the back." The man walked slowly back to the dock and down to the waiting boat. He unfastened the line and jumped aboard, giving the boat a shove off the dock. Then the driver put the engines in gear and moved off into the darkness. Rawls watched it go through his Night Sight before he relaxed.

He walked over to the case and played his flashlight over it. It was much the same as the first case, right down to the FedEx envelopes. He closed it, took it into the house, and dumped the contents onto the kitchen table.

He counted all of it again and came up with the sum of two million dollars, in fifties and hundreds. All he had to do now was figure out what to do with it.

22

Stone was at his desk the following morning when his secure cell phone rang. It wasn't Lance calling from a blocked number, so . . . "Hello, Ed."

"And a bright good morning to you," Rawls replied.

"You sound cheerful," Stone said. "Somebody must be dead."

"Well, you know . . ."

"Yeah, I heard all about it again on TV this morning."

"Have you heard anything that, maybe, wasn't on TV?"

Stone knew Ed was asking if he'd had any information from Dino. "If I had, I wouldn't be telling you."

"Of course not. I called for some financial advice."

"Okay. Are you playing with your own money?"

"I am. You introduced me to your financial

friend, Charley, a while back. Is he still in the game?"

"He is. More than ever. He, Mike Freeman, and I formed an investment partnership, Triangle Investments. Charley Fox handles the markets and the numbers, Mike and I try and come up with good buys among small companies and start-ups. We've done well."

"As you might imagine," Rawls said, "I've recently come into an, ah, inheritance."

"Frankly, I thought they wouldn't pay. I thought they would take you out instead."

"I considered that thought and took precautions. The transaction closed mostly as planned."

"And now you want to invest the proceeds?"

"Something like that. Can you give me Charley's number again?"

"I'd better speak to him first," Stone said. "What form is your investment going to take?"

"Cash: fifties and hundreds."

"Charley won't take that. You're going to have to do your laundry first."

"What form would please him?"

"A cashier's check from a reputable bank."

"Define 'reputable.'"

"One that doesn't take in Mob cash and

145

spit out stock in Apple."

"How about a nice, small-town Maine bank?"

"Sounds good."

"Have a word with Charley and get back to me on this line?"

"Sure."

"Bye." Ed hung up.

Stone called Charley.

"Triangle Investments."

"It's Stone."

"Hey, what's up?"

"I've got a . . . an acquaintance who would like to open an investment account with you. His name is Ed Rawls." Stone spelled it for him.

"Who is he?"

"Retired CIA, very smart."

"You recommend him?"

"I do."

"This isn't going to be cash, is it?"

"No. I mean, he could do that, but he says a cashier's check on a small-town Maine bank."

"Okay, tell him to call me."

"I will."

"Stone, is this one of those things that I shouldn't ask questions about?"

"Not unless you *really* want the answers."

"I've got just one: What's the source of

146

the money?"

"Asked that question, Ed would reply, 'From an inheritance.' "

"Oh."

"If you're nervous, Charley, turn it down. That won't get you into any trouble."

"It won't make any money for us, either."

"Good point."

"Okay, I'll talk to him."

"I think he would respond well, if you wanted to pick the investments without consulting him."

"I like that idea."

"Ed will call." Stone hung up.

Rawls hung up after a brief conversation with Charley. He put all the cash into a leather duffel, got into his Jeep and made the next ferry to Lincolnville, then he drove into Rockland, to a bank branch in a small shopping center. He entered the place and took a chair where he could see through the glass wall of the president's office. When the man finished his conversation and his visitor left, he saw Rawls and waved him in.

Rawls walked into his office, set down his duffel, and shook the man's hand. "How are you, Harvey?"

They exchanged some desultory chat, then the man said, "What can I do you for

147

today, Ed?"

"I'd like to purchase a cashier's check."

"Sure, in what amount?"

Rawls gave him a peace sign.

"Thou?"

Rawls shook his head.

"Mil?"

Ed nodded slightly.

"The green stuff?"

Ed nodded again.

"I'll need to have it counted and sorted. It will take a few minutes."

"Do you have one of those machines, Harvey?"

"I do."

Ed placed the duffel on his desk. "Count it yourself, will you? I don't want to become the subject of idle chat among your staff."

"Sure. Make yourself at home. Coffee?"

"Black, sugar."

Harvey picked up the duffel, said something to a woman at a desk outside, and she brought in a cup of coffee while Harvey repaired to a back room.

Twenty minutes later, Harvey came back with an envelope and the duffel, now empty. "The count was good; I ran it twice." He handed Rawls the envelope. "Here's your check."

Rawls inspected the check, then tucked

148

the envelope into a pocket and picked up his duffel.

"I'm supposed to ask you the source of the funds," Harvey said, "but I don't care much what you tell me."

"A long-lost uncle croaked at last and left it to me."

"I like that one," Harvey said. "What else can I do for you?"

"Nothin'."

"Give the coffee lady fifty bucks for the check, and you're out of here."

Rawls did so, and left. He drove around the corner to a FedEx shop, went inside, signed the check, and shipped it to Triangle Investments, for early delivery the next day.

Rawls drove back to Lincolnville, bought a Boston paper, and got in line for the ferry. In due course, he drove off the ferry, stopped at the Dark Harbor store, and picked up some ice cream. "Anybody new in town, Billy?" he asked the proprietor.

"A plumber feller from Searsport come over on the ferry before yours," Billy replied.

"Who would call all the way to Searsport for a plumber?"

"Beats me," Billy said. "Odd, that's what it is."

Rawls thanked him and got back into his Jeep. He drove down the road, checking every vehicle he saw, then past his own gate, before he turned around. He drove past the gate again, then pulled off the road, reached under the passenger seat, and pulled out a zippered leather pouch that produced a 9mm Colt and two extra magazines. He jammed a magazine into it, racked the slide, set the safety, and put it into an inside pocket, along with the spare magazine. He took the bag of ice cream in his left hand and walked across the road and into the weeds.

He'd take the shortcut to his house.

23

Rawls walked slowly through the tall weeds, careful not to make any noise. Presently, he drew even and within sight of his gate, which any intruder would be hard pressed to defeat. Parked there — engine running — was a van emblazoned with SEARSPORT PLUMBING. There was no one at the wheel, and Rawls assumed it to be empty.

He sat down behind a tree, with the van at his back, and got out his Agency iPhone, afraid that he would get no reply. Instead, "This is Jim."

"This is that other fellow," Rawls said. "Answer me a question, and tell me the truth: Do you or anybody you know have a connection with a firm called Searsport Plumbing, in Searsport, Maine."

"I don't," Jim said. "Let me check with others." He put Rawls on hold.

Rawls wished he had a spoon, so he could eat some ice cream.

Jim came back: "Neither I nor anyone at my place of business has a connection with a Searsport Plumbing. What, may I ask, is *your* connection with such an entity?"

"A van bearing that name is parked at my gate, empty, but with the engine running."

"And where are you?"

"Fifty yards from my house, parallel with the driveway."

"I have two suggestions for you," Jim said. "One: get out of there and lose yourself. Two: alternatively, shoot first and ask questions later. Anything else?"

"I'll call again, if I need to run."

Jim hung up.

Rawls resumed his travel toward his house, this time on his belly, being careful with the ice cream. Ten yards from his house, Rawls saw something move, then heard a boot strike his front porch.

"I can't figure out how to open the gate," a voice said. "You go back to the van and stay there until I come. Keep the engine running."

"Right," another voice replied.

Rawls knew he was going to have to make a decision now. As he watched the house, two men came into view simultaneously — one to his left walking up the driveway, the other from his front porch, carrying an exotic rifle.

Rawls didn't hesitate. He took aim and put a round into the nape of the rifle-bearer's neck. The man collapsed like a rag doll, but Rawls didn't wait to see him hit the ground. He turned ninety degrees to his left and found the other man in a firing crouch, a pistol in his hand. Rawls shot him in the face. "Stupid fuck," he muttered to himself. "You should have ducked for cover."

He had no doubt that both men were dead, but he checked anyway, then he opened the gate with his remote, got into the van and drove down the driveway. He stopped at the first body, then got out and loaded it into the rear bay, which was empty of any equipment. So much for any actual plumbing. He went to the second body and checked his face for familiarity. Nothing, and the first guy didn't have a face anymore. He went through the man's pockets, found a couple of passports, one Russian, one U.S., and a thick wad of cash. He pocketed the passports and the cash, then got the corpse over his shoulder and loaded into the van. A search of the first man's body yielded much the same as the other.

Rawls unreeled a length of hose from the side of the house, turned it on, and washed the blood off the driveway and the stones by the porch. Once cleaned up, he went into the house and had some ice cream, a little soft now. Then he turned on the TV and watched the news.

A moment after sundown, Rawls went down to his boathouse, where he had berthed an Army surplus amphibian personnel carrier of Korean War vintage, nicely restored. He used it to take large loads and the occasional car to and fro around Penobscot. Its troop bay would hold a twenty-five-foot boat. He used it to take his own boat to the yard for the winter. He started the amphib's engines, then drove it around to his dock and tied it stern to and perpendicular to the dock. That done, he opened the rear gates, then put the ramp down, so that it overlapped the floating dock and held the gates open.

He stepped onto the floating dock, then went back to the van, started it, and drove it slowly down the ramp to the floating pontoon. The tide was high, so there wasn't much of a slant. He drove the van onto the personnel carrier and set the brakes, leaving the gates open and the ramp down. He rolled both front windows all the way down, cast off the aft lines, then went forward to the driver's seat.

It was dark now. He looked around and saw no moving traffic in sight, then he put the engines into gear, and, at idle speed, moved it away from his dock and, slowly, out into Penobscot Bay, watching his depth sounder. At ninety feet of depth he took the engines out of gear and walked back to the van. He got the driver's door open wide enough to reach the controls, then he started the engine and put it in reverse, then hopped out and helped it along with a push. The vehicle rolled back, its weight tilting the carrier a good ten degrees. It was a front-wheel-drive vehicle, and it kept moving until it left the carrier and began to float. Rawls stood and watched it. It stayed afloat until enough water leaked through the frame to sink to the level of the window-sills. Once the water reached the sills, it began to pour into the van, and it sank fairly quickly. Shortly, it disappeared and the water became smooth again.

Rawls pulled in the ramp, closed the gates, and got back behind the wheel. Soon the carrier was tucked safely back in the boat-house, where he secured it, then went back to the house.

For dinner, he finished the ice cream. Once he wasn't hungry anymore, he checked the contents of the two men's pockets and found that they had been carrying five thousand dollars each, in hundreds. Plus they had a few hundred they must have had before they were hired.

He checked out the passports carefully, decided he had no need of them, and burned them to ash in the fireplace. Then he inspected the weapons carefully. They were both attractive, but he thought they might have been used previously, and he decided to put them into the bay the following morning.

Then, tired from his efforts, Rawls went to bed.

The following morning, his secure cell phone rang.

"Yes?"

"It's Jim. I wanted to see if you were still alive."

"I am, but the plumbers weren't so lucky."

"Did you clean up after them?"

"Of course." He told Jim about the passports.

"They probably used the U.S. ones to get into the country, but I think they would be dangerous to use again."

"I figured and took the proper steps."

"The plumbers were almost certainly Russian. I think that, when they don't report in, replacements will be sent to visit you."

"Then they'll meet the same fate."

"Then they'll send lots more. We think you should find a safe location for a while, preferably out of the country."

"That may be good advice."

"We can check the temperature from time to time and let you know when it's all right to return home."

"Good."

"Would you like the chopper to take you someplace near an international airport?"

"I would."

"It's not far away, and we can have it at 57 Bravo in, say, three quarters of an hour?"

"I'll be waiting for it."

"I'd suggest Teterboro; it won't be noticed there, and it's a cab ride to Newark or JFK."

"Teterboro is fine."

"Bon voyage." Jim hung up.

Ed starting packing his bags. The Russians' dollars would do him for walking-around money. He called a cab and opened the gate, then took the weapons down to the dock and flung them as far as he could.

He was all locked up and waiting on his porch when the cab arrived.

24

Rawls stood on the airstrip's ramp, awaiting the helicopter. He got out his secure iPhone and made a call.

"Ed? That you?" Stone asked.

"It is, though others didn't intend it to be so."

"Trouble?"

"Double trouble. Problem solved, but I've had strong advice to beat it. I know you have some property abroad. Can you put me up somewhere? I don't much mind where."

"I can offer you London — Belgravia — my house down in the country, on the Beaulieu River. Or Paris, off the Boulevard Saint-Germain."

"The English countryside sounds nice."

"Where are you now?"

"Waiting for a chopper at 57 Bravo, bound

for Teterboro."

"I'll call you back shortly."

Stone called Mike Freeman at Strategic Services. "What's up?" Mike asked.

"Have you got an airplane headed for England or northern Europe anytime soon?"

"I've got some people headed for London tomorrow morning. Wheels up at eight AM."

"That will work for my friend. His name is Ed Rawls."

"*That* Ed Rawls?"

"One and the same. He's been doing some freelancing for Langley, and it came back to bite him on the ass. He needs to get out."

"We'll be glad to have him," Mike said.

"I'll tell him to get a room nearby and to be there early tomorrow."

"Is somebody looking for him?"

"Could be."

"We've got two little apartments for crew in our hangar. He's welcome to one for the night. He can board the plane from inside tomorrow morning. Would it be helpful if we dropped him at your airstrip?"

"Perfect. I owe you yet another one."

The two men hung up and Stone called Rawls back. "Yeah?"

"At Teterboro, go to Jet Aviation and ask

the front desk where the Strategic Services hangar is. Get a cart over there and give your name to the manager of their flight department, whose name is Gary. He'll put you up for the night, then on the airplane in the hangar tomorrow morning, wheels up at eight. They'll land at my airstrip at the house, then continue to their destination. You'll be met at the strip by my property manager, Major Bugg, and the housekeeper will see to your needs. Stay as long as you like. Give me a call to let me know you made it."

"Got it. Thanks very much, Stone. Listen, I don't have any reason to think anybody's looking for you, but I didn't think anybody was looking for me, either, until they showed up. My advice is to watch your ass."

They hung up, and Rawls could hear the chop of the helicopter rotor coming. A couple of minutes later he had tossed his bags into the chopper and it was climbing out of Islesboro.

At Teterboro he was driven to the Strategic Services hangar in an electric cart, and there Gary met him and sent him up a flight of stairs, where he would have a view of a half dozen airplanes in the hangar.

Gary pointed at the biggest airplane.

160

"Board the G-600 over there at seven-thirty; you'll have breakfast and lunch aboard. What do you eat for breakfast and what newspaper do you read?

"Scrambled eggs and sausages, and the *Times* will do just fine."

A groundsman took his bags and led him up the stairs to a snug sitting room and bedroom, with lots of airplane memorabilia scattered about. "Bathroom's in there," the man said, pointing. "I've been told to tell you that you shouldn't take any firearms. If you've got 'em, leave them with Gary for safekeeping. Customs from Southampton Airport will meet you on the Barrington strip. There's customs forms in the desk there. If you're carrying more than five grand in cash or negotiable instruments, you'll need to fill out one and hand it to the crew when you board, along with your passport."

"Gotcha," Rawls replied, and the man left him alone.

He turned on the TV to CNN and settled into a reclining chair, with his 9mm on the table next to him.

Stone hung up the phone and turned to Rocky. "Feel like a trip to England?"

"On your airplane?"

161

"On one even nicer."

"Sure."

"Somebody had a go at Ed Rawls, and he suggested we take a trip." He called Mike Freeman and signed them up.

"Your life is so much more interesting than mine," she said. "I'd better call my people and let them know our plans."

"Wait until we're in England, and present them with a fait accompli."

Rawls had just been relieved of his 9mm and seated on the G-600, when Stone Barrington and Rocky Hardwick appeared and joined him.

"We decided to take your advice," Stone said.

"Glad to have you aboard."

The hangar doors were opened, and the airplane began to be towed by a tractor. They were disconnected on the ramp, and several other people boarded the airplane.

"Those are Strategic Services people," Stone explained. "We're their guests."

A stewardess approached. "You might be more comfortable in the aft cabin," she said to them. "This crowd can get noisy after a couple of drinks."

They followed her to the aft cabin, which was peaceful with the door closed. The

162

engines started, and shortly the airplane began to taxi.

It was still daylight in the early evening when they set down on the strip at Windward Hall and were met by Major Bugg in a large golf cart. Rocky and Rawls were introduced. Customs was a formality.

"How long is the strip?" Rawls asked.

"Seven thousand feet," Stone replied.

"What the hell is it doing here?"

"It was built during the Second World War, when the RAF requisitioned the property for the duration. The intelligence services used it for light-aircraft air drops — weapons and operatives, in France and northern Europe. When the war was over and the family got the estate back, the strip was in good shape, and they kept it that way. Lucky for me."

Rawls was shown to a handsome room and told that dinner would be served in an hour in the library, drinks in thirty minutes.

They met, refreshed, in the library. "Stone," Rawls said, sipping a single malt Scotch, "This is very beautiful."

"It came my way through the good offices of Felicity Devonshire," Stone said. "She is currently the director of MI6, and she has a

163

house across the river," he explained to Rocky.

"I remember her well and fondly," Rawls said.

"Is there anything you need for your stay?"

"Are there any weapons here?"

Stone pointed to a corner of the room. "There's a rack concealed there, and there is a matched pair of Purdey 12-bores and shells here. Treat them nicely."

"I hope I won't need them," Rawls said.

25

After a dinner of roast pork and a fine claret, they gathered around the fireplace for brandy.

"Have you reported in?" Stone asked Rawls.

"I don't report," Rawls replied. "It's safer that way."

"Have you any idea how those plumbers found you at home?"

"One or two, neither of them very convincing or attractive."

"Do you think the Russians have somebody on the inside at the Agency?"

"Have you told anybody there about coming to England?"

"No," Stone said, "but Rocky will report in tomorrow."

"Rocky," Rawls said, "can you avoid that without getting into trouble?"

"It's easily avoided," Rocky said. "I just won't make the call. Trouble might happen later, but I'll have a good excuse."

"Their having somebody on the inside is the least attractive of my ideas, but if it's valid, then none of us should talk to anybody. That's not to say they can't track us down, if they're willing to spend money and staff time."

"Well," Stone said, "it's too late to pull the cards on our cell phones. The computer will already have located all three of us."

"Yeah," Rawls replied, "but if they have somebody inside, he won't necessarily have access to that computer; he could just be listening to conversations. Stone, do you have any private security here?"

"Not on a standing basis, but Mike Freeman could have people here by morning, if I ask."

"Who pays for that?"

"I do. But I can try to get Lance to go for it later, if events prove that it was necessary."

"Well," Rawls said, "if I had your money, I'd call Mike Freeman."

Stone left the room and did so, then returned. "There'll be six people here by breakfast, and they'll work round the clock."

"Then I'll feel better by breakfast. How do you entertain yourself here?"

"Unless you'd like to invite somebody,

there's reading, skeet shooting, riding, and television," Stone replied. "We get U.S., British, and European satellite services."

"That should keep me in old movies," Rawls said. He stood up. "Well, if you'll excuse me, I need to go sleep off some jet lag. It's a beautiful room, by the way. Thanks." He polished off his brandy and left the room.

"And now what will we do?" Rocky asked.

"I don't know," Stone replied, "but let's do it upstairs."

"Good idea."

26

The three did not meet again until lunch, which they had in the garden.

"What did you two do this morning?" Rawls asked.

"Well," Stone said, "first, I spoke to Lance."

"You called him? Was that a good idea?"

"He called me."

"He knows where we are?"

"He claims to," Stone replied. "We'll know for sure around cocktail time."

"Why then?"

"Because that's when Lance will arrive, if he knows where we are."

"Where's your money on that bet?"

"On Lance," Stone said.

"So, he's using the resources of the Agency to track you?"

"I think that's a safe bet."

"Were you using your secure cell phone?"

"That's the number he called me on."

"In theory, Lance shouldn't be able to track that phone."

"I don't think Lance subscribes to that theory."

"Ed," Rocky interjected, "do you think Lance would give a phone he couldn't track to one of his own people?"

"Point won," Rawls said. "So, what did you do after you talked to Lance?"

"I called Felicity Devonshire and invited her to dinner."

"She's good company."

"She is. More important, both she and Lance would be offended if we had only one other woman seated. I've been trying to think of one to offset you, but nothing so far."

"Perhaps I can help you out with that," Rawls said.

"Are you acquainted with a woman within dinner distance?"

"I am, if she can stay overnight?"

"In your room?"

"That remains to be negotiated," Rawls said.

"We can accommodate her, whether you win or lose."

"I'll call her," Rawls said, rising and producing his phone. He walked some distance from their table, made a call, and returned. "She'll be here at five, to give her time to freshen up."

"Tell us about her," Stone said.

"Her name is Sarah Deerfield — Dame Sarah, since her recent retirement as chief of the Metropolitan Police, in London. I think I'll let you discover the rest directly from the source."

"As you wish," Stone said. "We'll give her the room next to yours, so there'll be less distance to negotiate. Oh, I should have told you: we'll be black tie; you might let your dame know."

"Will do. I didn't bring a tuxedo, but I happen to have a black suit and a tuxedo shirt."

"That will do nicely."

"Did you two leave the house this morning?" Rawls said.

"Yes, we went for a ride. Do you ride, Ed?"

"Well, starting when I was fifteen, I spent three summers on a Wyoming ranch, and I learned to cowboy."

"Well, this afternoon, pick yourself out a horse. I believe we even have some western tack, if you prefer it."

"I'll wait to see if Sarah will join me tomorrow. And I can handle English tack, thank you, though I wouldn't like to do any roping with it."

"We shot skeet this morning, Ed, after our ride," Rocky said, finally answering his question. "Didn't you hear the gunfire?"

"I would expect to hear some gunfire on an English estate, so the sound of shotguns doesn't disturb me, unless they're sawn-off."

"Don't shoot skeet with Rocky," Stone said. "She doesn't miss. It gets to be boring after a while."

"Well, you missed only once," she said.

"I always miss the first pigeon, then I get better."

Stone was at the airstrip with the golf cart at half past five, already dressed for dinner. He had been there less than a minute when he spotted a private jet turning onto final approach. Shortly, it was on the ground, and Stone identified it as a Citation Longitude, the biggest Cessna currently being manufactured. He glanced toward the house and saw a Range Rover pull up and disgorge a woman dressed in a tight sweater, tight jeans, and cowboy boots. She was led into the house. Not what he had expected of a dame. He turned his attention back to the airplane. It should not have surprised him to see Lance step off the airplane already in black tie, too. His luggage was loaded onto

171

the cart, and they drove up to the house.

"Where have you come from, Lance?" Stone asked.

"Paris, of course. You should have known I'd take advantage of your hospitality."

"I guessed. Whose is the Longitude?"

"The Agency shares it with another one or two. I use it as often as I can to keep it out of their clutches."

They reached the front door of the house, left the cart and Lance's luggage to others, and went directly to the library. Rocky and Ed sat in comfortable chairs with drinks, waiting.

"I believe we're short a couple of ladies," Rocky said.

"I believe that Dame Sarah is upstairs, changing, and Dame Felicity arrives by boat, and the cart is on the way to meet her."

"Thank you, yes, Stone," Lance said. "I *would* like a single malt — whatever you have — over ice."

"Was I neglecting you, Lance?" Stone asked, picking up a bottle of Laphroaig and pouring a slug of it on rocks.

Stone poured himself one, in celebration of being on that side of the Atlantic, and joined the group.

"Where are Dino and Viv?" Lance said. "I

172

had thought you were all joined at the hip."

"We left on short notice," Stone said, "and they couldn't get free that quickly."

"Ah."

The door opened and Dame Sarah Deerfield entered, practically spilling out of a low-cut black dress, the look offset by snow-white hair. The men leapt to their feet and Rawls did the honors.

"May I introduce my friend, Dame Sarah Deerfield?" he asked.

"Call me Sally," she said, shaking hands. "Almost everybody does," she said, with a BBC accent.

"May I get you something to drink?" Stone asked.

"A large bourbon on the rocks," she said.

Stone poured her a Knob Creek.

Sally had just settled in when Dame Felicity Devonshire bustled into the room. "Good evening, all," she said. Introductions were unnecessary, since she knew everyone present. "Dear Sally," she said, air-kissing. "What a nice surprise to see you here. I didn't know you knew Stone."

"I didn't, Felicity, until about three minutes ago. I'm here at the kind invitation of Ed."

"I'm so glad," Felicity said, taking an offered chair. "And I come bearing disturbing

173

tidings, I'm afraid."

That stopped the crowd in their tracks.

27

Stone spoke up. "Well, now that you have our attention, Felicity, do tell us all."

"I can't say that I know all," she said, "but on the boat, crossing the Beaulieu River, I had a call telling me that our late acquaintances, the Pentkovskys, have been replaced by a gentleman called 'Serge the Greek.' Or sometimes, just 'The Greek.' "

Everyone stared blankly at her.

"Oh, none of you know who that is, do you? I'm so relieved. I thought I was going to be the only one who'd never heard of him."

"I've heard of him," Lance said, blithely. "I just don't quite understand who he is. And I must say, it seems odd that the Russian Mob should take a Greek as their leader."

"Oh, he's only half Greek," Felicity replied. "His mother was all Greek."

"Thank you for clearing that up," Lance

said. "Now, who the hell is he?"

"One doesn't know, does one?"

"Really, Felicity," Stone said. "It's unlike you to come to dinner uninformed."

"Well, I'm at least as informed as anyone else here. Apparently." She paused for a sip of her martini. "Oh, I was also informed that he worked his way to the top level of the Russian Mob as an assassin. There, that's every bit of what I know."

"That's very unsatisfying," Lance said, producing an iPhone and typing furiously with his thumbs for half a minute. "There, we'll know more shortly."

"Oh, I've got my people on it, too," Felicity said.

"Of course you have," Lance replied.

The butler entered the room. "My Lords and Ladies," he intoned. "Dinner is served in the small dining room. If you will come this way." He led them down the hallway and pushed open the double doors, where a candlelit table awaited them.

While they were being seated, Stone said quietly to the butler, "Geoffrey, for future reference, we have two Ladies present, but no lords. All of the gentlemen are American."

"I was misinformed, Mr. Barrington. My apologies." He left the room.

176

"I wonder," Lance said, "if Geoffrey has been tasting the wines a bit too enthusiastically."

"Entirely possible," Stone said. "I would, in his place."

They dined on three courses, omitting the fish, and there was some tension in the room because no one's phone rang. They were back in the library with their port and brandy before Lance's phone made a noise, followed immediately by Felicity's. They both consulted their screens.

Lance cleared his throat, and they all turned toward him. "I'm very much afraid," he said, "that the American intelligence community has nothing on a Serge the Greek." He turned to Felicity. "How did your people do?"

Felicity shook her head. "Nothing," she said. "Absolutely nothing."

Stone blinked. "I wouldn't have thought it possible," he said, "that neither of your firms . . ."

"It's *not* possible," Lance said. "It's just very peculiar."

"*Most* peculiar," Felicity echoed.

Everyone sat quietly for a minute or so. Finally, Ed Rawls broke the silence. "May I offer a suggestion?" he asked.

"Please do," Felicity replied.

"I expect that the files of both your firms are, or rather, were, bursting with information on Mr. Greek. It appears that someone has been at your computers and done some erasing."

"That is an alarming possibility," Lance said, "but, nevertheless, an intriguing one."

"I suggest," Ed said, "that you have your people consult your backup files."

"If someone has erased his files," Stone said, "wouldn't he also erase the backups?"

"Not necessarily," Ed replied. "The Agency's last-ditch files are hard copies, and they are tucked away in a former mine somewhere in the western United States. Is that not so, Lance?"

Lance drew a deep breath and heaved a sigh. "It is so, but I'm not sure how recent the most recent files are."

"Time to find out," Ed said.

Lance's thumbs went to work again, and he got an answer almost immediately. He put his phone away. "Sometime tomorrow," he said. "Perhaps the day after."

"Felicity?" Stone said. "You don't seem to be sending any requests to search the tucked away hard copies."

"I'm afraid," she said, "we don't have any hard copies tucked away."

"I am shocked," Lance said, not sounding shocked, "but not surprised. Our British cousins have, for some time, enjoyed lording over us our reliance on nonelectronic storage systems, which they perceive not as archival, but as archaic. Perhaps they will now see the error of their ways."

"Perhaps," Dame Felicity said, "but perhaps not."

Stone snuck a glance at his watch. "Felicity, may we offer you shelter for the night?"

"Thank you, Stone. It has begun to rain, and the river is unpleasant in an open boat under those circumstances."

Stone had already reserved the room next to Lance's for her, but he left her to search it out, suspecting that she might find Lance's room along the way. Rawls and Sally Deerfield were looking very chummy, too. Presently, they all went up to bed.

"What are the sleeping arrangements?" Rocky asked as they were undressing.

"In my arms," Stone replied.

"Not us: the others."

"I will leave them to sort that out for themselves. Each of the guest rooms are furnished with bedclothes and dressing gowns."

"I did notice Felicity casting a hungry look

at Lance a couple of times . . ."

"So did I," Stone said, climbing into the bed.

"But Lance wasn't returning them."

"It is part of Lance's makeup that he does not wish others to know what he does or what he thinks, unless he chooses to be revealing. Tonight, he has chosen to reveal nothing."

"Whereas I," she said, climbing in naked beside him, "choose to reveal everything."

"And lovely it is in the moonlight," Stone said, reaching for her.

"I noticed that you have not observed the British tendency to close the curtains at dusk."

"The moonlight is why I have not," he said, kissing her on a breast.

"I didn't say anything earlier," Rocky said, "but I have heard a few things about Serge the Greek."

Stone curtailed his activities and sat up in his bed. "Tell me," he said.

So Rocky told him about Serge the Greek.

28

Rocky sat up, too. "Serge the Greek has been, for the past few years, very close to Pentkovsky the younger, while being despised by Pentkovsky the elder. Night or day, Serge has never been far from the elbow of Anton. They were classmates at the GRU academy, and the nature of their relationship was formed there."

"And what was that nature?"

"Likely, but not certainly homoerotic," she said. "Neither of them, while appearing often in public with women, was known to have any lasting relationship with a member of the opposite gender. But other parts of their relationship were established in those early days at their academy. Anton as the dominant and Serge as the slightly submissive."

" 'Slightly submissive'?"

"While Anton was the boss, Serge never did anything that, even for a moment, would

181

have made him look submissive. There are people, now dead, who made the mistake of commenting on their relationship in his hearing."

"Touchy on that subject, was he?"

"To the extreme."

"Tell me," Stone said. "If Serge was always at Anton's elbow, where was he at Hong Fat, when Ed Rawls blew Anton's brains out?"

"In the kitchen," Rocky replied. "Serge is a keen cook, and he asked the management if he could watch the chef preparing their dinners. Ed chose that moment to get his rounds off, and since he was using a silenced weapon, Serge did not immediately notice what was happening, because of the clattering of pots, pans, and dishes. But a few seconds later, the screams from the dining room caught his attention. By that time, Ed was out of there. When Serge emerged from the kitchen and viewed the carnage, he had two ways to try and catch up with the killer, and he chose the wrong one, giving Rawls all the time he needed to depart the neighborhood."

"How did you acquire this knowledge?"

"I serve with a small division of the Agency, which we and others sometimes call 'the Pod.' We pursue our own cases and operations, and have sources of various kinds of information exclusive to us. Lance pays little attention, unless he needs something we specialize in."

"And what does the Pod specialize in?"

"I'm afraid I have already revealed more than I had intended to. It's best that I reveal no more, unless it becomes clear to me that the knowledge is needed."

"So now you're going to clam up?"

"I have already done so. Now," she said, "where were we?"

They quickly found their place.

Early in the morning the *whir* of the electric cart could be heard from the forecourt, and Stone looked out the window in time to see Felicity depart in it for the dock and her boat.

"Anything interesting?" Rocky asked, rolling over.

"Just Felicity leaving, but we can't know from which room."

"I got tiny vibes from her," Rocky said, "that made me think she has almost as much interest in women as in men."

"You are not mistaken," Stone said. "And you should be careful, while being nice to her, not to encourage her in that direction, unless you, too, are interested."

"I am not."

"Then never let her think that you might be, or one morning, you'll wake up with her in your bed."

"She's head of MI5, is she?"

"No, MI6, the foreign branch. MI5 is more like our FBI, dealing with domestic matters."

They stopped talking.

"What is that noise?" Rocky asked.

"That was the sound of one or more men in boots running through the gravel of the driveway," Stone said, getting up and heading for his dressing room.

"Shall I come?"

"No, I'm expected to take an interest, and as soon as I have, I'll come back for breakfast."

Stone finished dressing and left the room without another word. He ran lightly down the stairs, almost colliding with Major Bugg, the estate manager, on his way up.

"What's wrong?" Stone asked.

"Trouble," Bugg said, panting a little. "One of the Strategic Services men has been found dead, with a knife wound to his throat."

"Then you'd better call Chief Inspector Holmes," Stone said.

"I have already done so."

"And call Dame Felicity's house and inquire of her health from one of the staff."

Stone went to the library and debated with himself whether to call Mike Freeman at this hour and wake him up, or wait until later. He called the number.

"What?" Mike said.

"It's Stone. Bad news. One of your people from your London station was knifed last night and is dead. The police are on their way."

"I'll send my station chief, Philip Charter, down from London. Do you know him?"

"We met once, I think. We'll be ready for him."

"I know those men well," Mike said. "Not just anybody could get a knife into any of them without suffering serious damage himself. See if you can find another body, or evidence of a wounding."

"Certainly."

"Philip is a Brit. He commanded the Special Air Service, before he retired."

"Good to know."

"Don't try to keep anything from him or ease the blow."

"Got it." The two men hung up.

Stone went outside and waited on the front steps for the Hampshire constabulary to show up. They didn't take long.

185

Inspector Holmes got out of the Range Rover, walked to where Stone stood, shook his hand. "Tell me everything," he said.

Stone told him what he knew and some of the background, while Holmes nodded and walked quickly with him down the drive toward the river, where Major Bugg stood by a lump under a blanket.

"Dame Felicity is safe in her bed," he said to Stone. "We didn't wake her."

"How is Dame Felicity involved?" Holmes asked.

"She isn't. She was here for dinner last night and left the house about sunrise."

"Is this where you found the body?" Holmes asked Bugg.

"Yes, one of his colleagues found it around seven AM."

"Then the murderer wouldn't have collided with Dame Felicity," Holmes said.

"It could have been close," Stone said.

Holmes turned to one of his men. "I want a body temperature," he said. "Don't wait for the medical examiner."

29

At mid-morning, Colonel Philip Charter got out of a large Mercedes SUV. Stone saw him coming and greeted him on the front steps. "Good morning, Colonel," Stone said. "I'm Stone Barrington." Charter was smaller than Stone, about five-nine, he reckoned, and very trim and fit-looking, appearing to be in his early fifties, with thick gray hair trimmed fairly short.

"Good morning, Mr. Barrington," he replied, offering his hand. "May I see the body of my colleague?"

Stone drove him there in the cart. Charter whipped away the blanket and examined the man thoroughly, front and back. While they were there, the medical examiner arrived in his van and conducted his own examination. "Dead around three hours," he said. "Apparent cause of death, exsanguination, as the result of a wound to the artery, applied from behind."

"I would have thought that impossible," Charter said, "knowing the man and his capabilities."

The ME gently rolled him over. "Ah, the knife wasn't his first wound," he said. "He was shot from behind at the base of the skull, a small-caliber round, probably a .22. He would have expired virtually instantly, knowing nothing. The knife wound was merely an insult."

Charter grimaced. "Which will be repaid in full."

"Come back to the house, and let's talk," Stone said.

Charter refused to move until his colleague's body had been carefully put on a stretcher and placed in the van, then he got back into the cart.

Neither of the two men spoke again until they were comfortably seated in the library and had been served coffee.

"Are you sure you wouldn't like breakfast?" Stone asked.

"I seem to have lost my appetite," Charter replied.

"Colonel . . . ?"

"Please call me Philip, all my equals do. My inferiors and superiors call me Colonel."

Stone was pleased to be thought of as the man's equal, though he was not sure that was true. "Philip, I'm a former homicide detective with the New York Police Department, and I can assure that the work of both Inspector Holmes and the ME was properly conducted."

"Thank you. I made a couple of phone calls on the way down here, and, as a result, I have some information on the likely killers." He repeated largely what Stone already knew.

"What were your sources for this information?"

"The Metropolitan Police and an elite unit of your CIA, known as the Pod."

Stone smiled. "The recently retired chief of the Metropolitan Police dined here last evening, and a member of the Pod is upstairs, either sleeping or dressing."

"Ah, Dame Sally!" Charter said. "Quite a dish, isn't she?"

"Quite."

"And the other?"

"Her name is Rocky Hardwick. Her chief, Lance Cabot, is also upstairs, but he may prefer not to make an appearance. In any case, he knew nothing about this Greek fellow. He's still awaiting the result of a search of his dead files. Also, Dame Felicity Devonshire was here for dinner and knew nothing more than the name, no details."

"Makes you wonder what these intelligence people do with their time, doesn't it?"

"In their favor, the subject is a rather obscure figure."

"I'll give them that. I intend to know everything there is to know about him and his before I'm finished."

"Our presence here is the direct result of their attempts on my life," Stone said, "so I will be happy to hear of anything bad that happens to them."

Charter smiled, the first time he had done so. "If you don't mind, I will accept your invitation to breakfast."

Stone rang for the butler and they gave their orders.

"What is your background?" Charter asked over his omelet.

"New York University, the law school there, and fourteen years with the NYPD. I was invalided out after a bullet to the knee, though that was more of an excuse than a cause. I've practiced law since then with the New York firm of Woodman & Weld. What about you?"

"Eton, Sandhurst, the Army; that's it, until I got a call from Mike Freeman one day, shortly after I retired. As it turned out, I

190

wasn't retired for long."

"Mike is a good man. I've served as his corporate counsel and now, for some years, on his board. We've partnered in some investments, too."

"Those are good credentials. I'm glad not to be dealing with some corporate type."

"I don't think anyone has ever thought me that," Stone replied.

Rocky entered the room and was invited to join them.

Stone introduced Colonel Charter.

"I had breakfast in bed, but I'll have another cup of coffee," she said. "Colonel, I'm told you've been in touch with some of my people."

"I have, and they were very helpful. Please call me Philip, and I'll call you Rocky, if I may."

"Of course."

"Is your name short for something?"

"Roxanne, which I despise."

Inspector Holmes entered and was asked to join them.

"I'm afraid I have work to do," he said. "Colonel, is there a family I should contact?"

"Our company is his family," Charter replied.

"And what disposition of his remains do you wish?"

"The military hospital at Sandhurst; I've already made the arrangements."

"Of course. I'll be off then. Gentlemen. Ms. Hardwick." He departed.

"He doesn't appear to be an oaf," Charter said.

"Don't underestimate him," Stone replied.

"I'll remember. I've got another four men arriving shortly," he said.

"In light of what's happened," Stone said, "we can use them."

"Once I've briefed and made disposition of them, my work here will be done. I'll go back to London and start pursuing the Greek."

"I'd like your opinion on whether we should remain at this house, or move, in the circumstances."

"I understand you have other houses," Charter said, "but I don't have an opinion on whether you'd be safer here or at one of them."

"Then I think we'll stay on for a bit longer," Stone said.

"Is there anything you need that I can provide?"

"Perhaps some handguns, and a long rifle or two."

"I'll have my men see to that and provide ammunition, as well."

"I think we'll feel safer armed," Stone said.

"One usually does, doesn't one?"

30

Charter went out to meet with his men, leaving Stone and Rocky alone.

"Heard anything from Lance this morning?" she asked.

"I never know whether Lance is breakfasting in bed, sleeping, or working," Stone replied. "When he's staying with us he generally turns up around lunchtime."

To his surprise, Lance entered the room, dressed in tweeds, flannels, and a shirt open at the neck, a walking statement of informality.

"Good morning," Lance said, then sat down, shook out a napkin, and poured himself a cup of coffee.

"Did you sleep well?" Stone asked.

"No," Lance replied. "I was awakened in the middle of the night by people from my office."

"That must have been important," Stone said.

"I must ask both of you not to use your Agency cell phones. Also, please remove the data card from each."

"Are we being tracked?" Rocky asked.

"Worse than that," Lance replied, then went silent.

Stone figured he'd tell them when he was ready and left him alone. So did Rocky.

"Lovely day out there," Lance said. "Perhaps I'll take a walk before lunch."

"Perhaps you shouldn't," Stone said. "Have you heard about our fatality?"

Lance put down his coffee cup and stared at Stone. *What?*

Stone had forgotten that Lance preferred delivering news to receiving it from others. "One of our security team: shot with a small-caliber weapon, probably silenced, then his throat cut, unnecessarily." Quickly Stone summarized the rest of the morning — the appearance of Colonel Charter and Inspector Holmes, and the advice and resources he'd gained from Charter.

"This is what comes of turning off my cell phone," Lance said, as if he had caused the murder to happen.

Stone remembered that he had been told to disable his own phone, and he did so. Rocky followed.

"Now we're deaf," she said.

195

"May we use the landline?" Stone asked.

"How many lines do you have?" Lance asked.

"Six, I think."

"Please ask Major Bugg to order two new lines to be installed today. Keep the phone numbers secret from anyone but Major Bugg and us."

"Do you think our lines are tapped?" Stone asked.

"It's a reasonable assumption," Lance said. "I can only hope that they're not tapped at the exchange, or the new one will be worthless."

"I can ask the police to help with that," Stone said.

"Please do so," Lance replied. "And I should tell you, Stone, that henceforth you and Ed are not to be regarded as the only potential victims. I've been given to understand that the Greek dispenses revenge with a broad brush, so none of us is safe. We should travel, if we must, in pairs, and be armed at all times. I'll help myself from the small armory provided by Colonel Charter."

"I take it you know the Colonel?"

"Better than I wish to," Lance replied. "He's a good fellow, but an unpredictable one. And having lost a man, there's no telling what steps he might take."

196

"He gave me that impression," Stone said. "I think someone out there can look forward to having his throat cut."

"Indeed," Lance replied.

"I'd better speak to Major Bugg about the phones," Stone said, rising, but was stopped by the entrance of that gentleman, who greeted them all.

"Major," Stone said, "we're going to require a new telephone line — make that two — at the earliest possible moment, the numbers to be a closely held secret."

Bugg nodded and tapped his ear, questioningly. Stone nodded, then held up his cell phone and made a cutting motion across his neck with a finger.

Bugg turned to leave. "Ask for Holmes's help with the exchange, if needed," Stone called to him before he closed the door.

"I need a place somewhere in the house where I can work," Lance said.

Stone nodded. "My son and his partner made a film here shortly after I bought the place. We made a suite of offices for their use, well-equipped, on the lowest level, southeastern corner. It's all still there, in case they ever come back. There's a multi-line phone system; ask Bugg to dedicate a line for your use."

"Right." Lance stood.

"What about our ordinary cell phones; are they usable?"

"Perhaps, but only for mundane purposes. Yield no information, certainly not about our location or what we've learned about the Greek, and turn them completely off when you're not calling or checking for incoming calls. And don't forget to check your phone messages and e-mails frequently."

"Understood," Stone said, and Lance left.

"Is there such a thing in Britain as a throwaway phone?" Rocky asked.

"I don't know," Stone said. "I'll ask Charter. Let's go find him." They walked outside to the front steps and looked around: no sign of Charter or his men. "Let's walk back to the stables," Stone said. "If they're any good, they'll find us." He led the way. As they turned the corner of the house, someone fell in behind them.

Stone turned and looked at the man; one of Charter's. "Do you know where I can find the Colonel?" he asked the man.

"One moment, sir," the man replied. He produced a small handheld radio and spoke into it. "He's in the stables," the man said to Stone. "Straight ahead." Stone led the way, and a moment later, when he looked back, the man had disappeared.

They found Charter in a stall, where a table and a chair had been set up. "Good morning again," he said. "What can we do for you?"

"Do shops in England sell throwaway cell phones?" Stone asked him.

Charter reached under his table and produced a cardboard box. "Is two each enough?" he asked, taking them from the box and setting them on the table.

"I should think so. Can you send a couple to Lance Cabot? He's working on the lower level of the house, southeast corner."

"Of course." A man appeared from nowhere, as if by intuition, and Charter handed him the phones and gave him his instructions, then he turned back to his table. "Anything else I can do for you?"

"Thank you, no."

"Then I suggest you take the phones inside and stay there, away from the windows."

Having been dismissed, they took their phones and left. They settled into the library, and Stone used one of his new phones to call Dino.

"Bacchetti."

"Not too early for you, I hope."

"Nope. Where the hell are you? You haven't been answering your phone."

Stone explained the circumstances and brought him up to date.

"You'd better stay where you are," Dino said. "Wherever that is, it's safer than here."

"Perhaps things are better in a green and pleasant place," Stone said. "Or would be, if we hadn't had the fatality early this morning."

"You didn't mention that."

"I did, just now. Don't rush me."

"Just stay there, pal, and be careful."

"Maybe, we'll see." They said goodbye and hung up.

"Dino thinks we should stay here," Stone said to Rocky.

"Maybe he's right."

"Maybe I should send for my airplane, instead of waiting for the next Strategic Services airplane."

"Do you think that would make us invulnerable?" she asked.

"Not being where we lost a man this morning could make us less vulnerable."

"Did you ever hear of a rocket-propelled grenade, RPG, for short?"

"Yes."

"It's a small weapon, but it can blow an airplane out of the sky."

"So, you're thinking it's safer here."

"We're here, and we're not dead."

"I can't argue with that logic," Stone said "Now that I think of it, maybe we shouldn't have been shooting skeet yesterday."

"At lease we were armed," she said.

"There is that," Stone admitted. "Maybe we should take Philip Charter's advice and just stay inside, away from the windows."

"That limits our choice of entertainment to reading, TV, or sex."

"I like all three, and my library is at your disposal."

"I'll read until I can't stand it anymore, then I'll attack you," she said.

31

In the absence of Dame Felicity, Stone had decreed no dinner dress, only suits, or as the British preferred to call them, "lounge suits."

Lance had shown up in as near as he could get to dinner dress, an almost-black suit and a pin-dotted necktie and not-quite-matching pocket square. Lance, who normally operated with a bland countenance, looked positively gloomy.

Stone didn't ask him what was the matter, but Lance told him anyway, while the others listened in.

"It's worse than the NSA thought," Lance said. "They've not only breached our encrypted phones, they've come up with their own network, with their own encryption."

Rawls was the first to grasp what he was saying. "That's not possible," he said. "No criminal gang has the resources and computer power to accomplish that. Only a nation-state, and a prosperous one at that, or one willing to dedicate a huge part of their economy to the task, could do it."

"I'm inclined to agree, Ed," Lance said. "And so is the NSA."

Stone finally saw a glimpse of dawn. "Do you mean that the Russian government has turned over a huge chunk of its capabilities to a bunch of thugs?"

Colonel Charter spoke up. "I think this just confirms what some of us have always believed — that the Russian government *is* a bunch of thugs."

"I'm just a retired copper," Sally Deerfield said. "Will someone tell me what you're talking about?"

"I think Philip has just told us," Stone said.

"Yes, but what does it *mean*?" Sally demanded.

"It means," Charter said, "that what we're up against is not just a band of brigands, but an army, and a well-financed and equipped one, at that."

"Lance," Stone said, now more sure of himself, "is our government going to be willing to match or, preferably, outmatch what we're up against?"

"I can tell you more about that after I've joined our president's daily intelligence briefing tomorrow morning, their time. For my part, I think we're fortunate to have the president we have, who has been schooled by the last two presidents to face something like this."

They were called to dinner. There wasn't much chatting at table, at first. Finally, Charter spoke up again.

"In the end," he said, "dealing properly with this situation is going to require an act of arms."

"In the end, certainly," Lance said. "What I'm worried about is the beginning, which directly concerns the people at this table."

From there, the conversation descended into geopolitics, something to which Stone had not given a lot of thought, and about which he had nothing to contribute.

After dinner, back in the library over brandy and coffee, Charter said to Lance, "May I speak to you privately?"

"Philip," Lance replied, with an edge in his voice. "We are all sentient grown-ups in this room, and we are all involved. So you may speak to all of us together."

Charter turned just the slightest bit red. "All right," he said, "right now I have fifteen men on the grounds, all of them ex-SAS. I can gather, perhaps, another twenty, not all of them employed by Strategic Services.

What I propose is a direct assault on every person on the grounds of this house who is not an employee of the estate or a guest here."

"Thank you for that, Philip," Stone said, drily. "I should hate for the house and staff to start taking mortar rounds. There's also the country hotel next door, which is full."

"Have no fear of that, Stone," Charter replied. "These people are no better equipped than my men are, with assault rifles and handguns. I propose to overwhelm them and kill as many as possible, perhaps taking a prisoner or two, whom I will interrogate personally."

"You propose to turn my wine cellar into a torture chamber?" Stone asked.

"There is no torture involved. Your own people have given it a more benign name: 'enhanced interrogation.'"

"Is that what you would like me to tell my president tomorrow?" Lance asked, drily.

"I do not propose that you tell your president anything," Charter said, "until it's over. Then you can give her glad tidings."

"There will be no glad tidings in anything I tell her if we follow your plan. There will be only consternation, followed by the sound of heads rolling down a White House corridor."

"Come now, Lance," Charter said. "You are dealing with a White House whose communications have been breached, only temporarily, of course. You would be within your rights to say nothing at that briefing, for fear it is reaching enemy ears."

"He has a point, Lance," said Ed Rawls, who had not spoken before then. "Suppose you tell her all these things at your briefing, and the Russians overhear all of it and choose to attack us first? Where will those of us in this room be then?"

"I'll give you this much, Philip," Lance said, glancing at his watch. "The briefing is scheduled for two pm tomorrow, our time; nine am at the White House. If you can recruit your men and be ready to present an assault plan at that time, I will present it to the president and, if I think it has a reasonable chance of success without starting an all-out war with the Sov . . . excuse me, Russians, I will endorse it."

"Let me see what I can do," Charter said.

Lance rose. "Then if you will all excuse me, I will take to my bed. Anything discussed in this room while I sleep, or try to, will have been said without my knowledge or participation. I trust you all to remember that at the subsequent congressional hearings. Good night." Lance departed the room.

Everyone looked at each other. Rawls spoke first. "I can plan murders, but not military assaults. Good night." He rose, and Sally rose with him. They left the room.

Charter turned toward Stone. "Well?"

"I have no military training or expertise to contribute," Stone said, "beyond the ability to fire a weapon at something I can see, so I don't believe I can be of any further use this evening." He stood. "Rocky, I'm turning in. You'll have to make your own decision."

Rocky stood. "I'll join you," she said, and they walked out, leaving Colonel Philip Charter to commune with his intellect and his conscience.

When they were in bed, Rocky said, "Do you think he'll do it?"

"I think that trying to predict what Philip Charter will do would be fruitless. I suppose we'll hear about it tomorrow, but all I can think of is this lovely house pockmarked with bullet holes and perhaps on fire."

"I cannot disagree," Rocky said.

"Then I propose that tomorrow morning, after a good breakfast, we get the hell out of here and head for London, where I have

207

shelter. I don't think this happy band of Russian assassins will attack the city."

"Neither do I," Rocky said. "I'll be packed and ready to go."

32

Stone and Rocky, in view of the impending action, decided to have breakfast downstairs with the others. They were mostly seated when Philip Charter came into the room, a little out of breath.

Stone was ready to tell him to stand down, but Charter beat him to it. "My men have just conducted a search of the grounds and the hotel next door, and it appears that the Russians have cleared out."

"That's a relief, Philip. What do you suggest we do now?"

"I suggest that, during what may be a lull, you travel to London, and we'll establish a perimeter around you at your house there."

"Ed? What say you?"

"I've already accepted an invitation from Sally to spend a few days at her house in Chelsea." He handed Stone a card. "This is her address and phone numbers."

Stone handed him his own card, and

Charter gave everybody his. He handed Stone a handheld radio. "We will follow you on the road. You can reach me on this or my cell phone on the trip north."

Stone thanked him and he and Rocky ate breakfast.

Ed and Sally left first, in her Range Rover. Stone and Rocky followed a few minutes later in his Porsche 911. They barely got their luggage in.

"How long a drive is it?" Rocky asked.

"An hour and a half, with decent traffic. Could take longer." They drove through the village and got onto the motorway.

"Do you see Charter's people anywhere?" Rocky asked.

Stone checked his mirrors. "I see a white SUV that could be him." He picked up the handheld. "Charter, this is Barrington. You there?"

"I'm a ways back."

"Are you driving a white SUV?"

"No, mine is black."

"Can you see me?"

"I could until a minute ago, but not now. Is your vehicle armored?"

"Only with speed," Stone replied.

"Hold your speed. I'll catch up."

Stone watched his mirrors; it took a

couple of minutes, then a black SUV was visible. "I see you," he said. "Do you see the white vehicle?"

"Yes, and I don't like the look of it. Get off at the next exit, go once around the roundabout, then get back on the motorway. Don't use your turn signals."

"Right. Exit coming up." Stone stayed in the center lane, then, at the last moment, swerved left into the exit. He did a 360 on the roundabout, then drove onto the motorway again.

"Good," Charter said. "We're ahead of you and behind the white vehicle. We'll pull up to him and get a look inside."

Stone watched from a couple hundred yards back as the black SUV pulled into the left lane and accelerated, pulling alongside the white vehicle. Stone was too far back to hear anything, but he saw Charter's vehicle swerve to the left again onto the stopping lane, then brake, seeming to fight for control, and pulled into the lane behind the white SUV again.

"Stone? Are you there?" Charter sounded agitated.

"I'm here."

"We took a shotgun round through the rear window. There's glass everywhere."

"I can see you both. The white car is ac-

211

celerating. Are you pursuing?"

"We're tagging him, but staying well back. Are you armed?"

Stone looked at Rocky, and she nodded. "I'm not. My companion is."

"Maintain your position; I'm calling the police on my cell."

Stone stayed well back. A couple of minutes later he saw a flashing blue light approaching the motorway ahead of him, then enter it. Behind him he saw another blue light approaching fast in the lane to his left, and it passed him like a rocket. "The cavalry is arriving," he said into the radio.

"Roger, I see them, and I'm in touch."

"Rocky," Stone said, "keep that weapon concealed and don't draw it, unless we're taking fire." Stone followed the flashing blue lights, but kept well back.

"What's the plan?" Rocky asked.

"I'm all out of plans, and I don't know what Charter's is. I'm just trying to keep them all in sight without getting arrested."

"That's a good plan," she said.

Stone noticed that it required 110 mph to keep the blue lights in sight.

"You aren't going to crash this thing at this speed, are you?" Rocky asked.

"Is your seat belt fastened?"

"A long time ago," she said.

"So is mine. Short of slowing down, we've done all we can."

"Are you considering that alternative?" she asked.

"Not yet. I want to see what happens."

"I'm not all that curious," she said. "I think I'd rather hear about it later."

"Oh, come on! Be a sport!"

"Assuming I could do that, I'd still be frightened."

Stone concentrated on staying in his lane, which had been cleared by the police car, and keeping the flashing blue lights in sight. Then something happened up ahead.

The white SUV veered to the right and appeared to cross over onto the southbound side of the motorway, against traffic. Then the white SUV seemed to rise into the air a couple of feet and turn onto its right side, then burst into flames.

Stone slammed on his brakes, in anticipation of what was happening ahead. Very quickly, the southbound lane was empty of traffic, then at 70 mph, they blew past the burning SUV on the northbound side of the motorway.

"Was that Charter?"

"No. Did you see that?"

"Yes, but I'm not sure what I saw."

"A cop pulled alongside the white SUV

and crowded it. The driver pulled right, then seemed to lose control. He struck the steel divider and rolled over into the southbound lane."

Charter called on the radio, "You okay?"

"Yes, we're intact and still heading north."

"How many in the vehicle?"

"Think I saw four, before the shotgun blast. I'm getting off at the upcoming exit to speak to the police. You continue as planned."

"Okay, will do." Traffic was moving freely again, since they had passed the burning vehicle, but the southbound lane had ground to a halt, and traffic was jamming up over there.

"Next stop, London," Stone said.

"That's okay with me," Rocky said. "I'm just glad we didn't get a closer look at the burning car."

"So am I," Stone said. "It can't have been a pretty sight."

33

Eventually Stone hit the London suburbs and had to slow for traffic and the fact that the roundabouts were closer together. He was in Ealing when Charter called again on the radio.

"I hear you, Philip," he said.

"All right. I've got a team at your house already, they're in Wilton Crescent and the housekeeper is helping them. They'll have your garage doors open when you arrive. Drive right in, and don't get out of the car until the doors are closed. I'll come in through the front door. I have a key."

"Good." Stone made his way to Wilton Crescent. There was an electric gate at the entrance to the mews, and he opened it with his remote and drove slowly down the cobblestones. He saw his garage door open and pulled inside, waiting for it to close. As it did, the lights came on, and he was greeted by the couple who ran the house,

Wilfred and Hilda, who dealt with the luggage while Stone and Rocky sat down for tea in the drawing room. A short while later, Charter entered and poured himself a cup from the service.

"All intact?" he asked.

"Sure. You're the one who caught the shotgun. Anyone hurt?"

"One man got a couple of pellets in the face. He's being attended to at a hospital."

"Don't the hospitals look at you askance when you walk in with a shotgun wound? Don't they call the police?"

"Not if you have the right ID," he said, waving a plastic-encased card. "I think they believe that Strategic Services is a government department, and I've no reason to enlighten them. They rounded up a plastic surgeon to deal with my man's face, so apart from some swelling, he'll be fine in a few days."

"Any further contact with the Greek's people?"

"No, and I hope he's running out of them." His radio squawked. "Yes?"

"Four men in a black Ford saloon car," a voice said.

"Do they seem to know where they're going?"

"I think they're looking for the Porsche.

We've moved the Range Rover out of the area."

"Let them look, then." Charter put down the radio. "It troubles me a bit that they're replacing men so quickly. Makes me wonder how many they have at their disposal."

"Do you have a theory as to how they got onto me?" Stone asked.

"The easy answer is they ID'd Ed Rawls and tracked him to your house in New York. I understand that you've had problems with them in the past, and that things went your way, not theirs. That would have irked them."

"I suppose so, but I'd be surprised if they could track Ed. He took precautions."

"What about you? What precautions were you taking?"

"Mostly just entering through the garage door, much as we did here."

"There's a very nice pub in the mews here," Charter said.

"Yes, the Grenadier; it's my favorite."

"Stay out of it. It's just the sort of place they'd hang out in to keep a watch on the house."

"I suppose so."

"We'll sweep the place and see if we can spot them and clean them out."

"Good. Are we going to be stuck in the

house while we're here?"

"That would be best. Your cook can do some shopping for you."

"Look, Philip, I think we'd be better off in New York."

"Your choice. I can't argue with that."

"I'll order my airplane to pick us up at London City Airport. The crew will arrive tomorrow, rest for the night, and we'll leave the day after."

"I'd suggest you use RAF Northam, instead. It has civilian facilities, and we have a base there, and it's mostly the M4 all the way. The South London suburbs are often jammed and could be a death trap."

"Okay, I'll pass that on to my pilot."

"I'll see what equipment is available for the transfer," Charter said, and left the room with his phone in his hand.

Stone used a throwaway to phone Ed Rawls. "Yeah?"

"It's Stone."

"I hear you had a little imbroglio on the motorway," he said.

"That was Charter. His car took a shotgun and one of his people was hit by some pellets."

"Hot around here, isn't it?"

"I was thinking of heading for more welcoming climes. To Teterboro the day after tomorrow. You up for that?"

"Can I bring Sally?"

"Sure, glad to have her."

"Me, too. Let me know where to meet you."

"We'll be flying out of RAF Northam, out the M4."

"I know it. I'll find your airplane."

"Let's aim for wheels up at noon."

"Okay."

"Talk to you later." They hung up.

Charter came back into the room. "We're set up for day after tomorrow. Tell your people to taxi to our hangar. The tower will direct them. That way you can board indoors."

"Sounds good. Wheels up at noon?"

"Very well. We'll pick you up in the mews at ten. I'll have a special vehicle for you."

"Rawls and Sally are meeting us there. Where shall I tell them to go?"

"Look for signs to Ace Aircraft Interiors. That's us. Come in the side door."

Stone got on the phone to New York and spoke to both Joan and Faith, who would arrange for a crew. He gave Faith instructions for landing and taxiing, then hung up.

One of Charter's people came in from the garage. "We've had a good look around the Grenadier," he said. "There are two likely culprits."

"Well, don't kill them if they're only likely," Charter said. "Our van will come into the mews the day after tomorrow at 09:45. See that they're occupied long enough for us to leave without their attention."

"Right."

Rocky, who had been listening to their conversations without commenting said, "Well, I guess a trip to Harrods is out."

"Good guess," Stone said. He called Rawls back to tell him about Ace Aircraft Interiors.

"What time will we get into Teterboro?" Rawls asked.

"Figure an eight-hour flight, depending on the headwinds. You and Sally are welcome to stay with me. We might do better if we're all together."

"I guess that's so," Rawls said.

"Ed," Stone said, "I'm glad you'll be along. We might need somebody shot."

"I'm your man," Rawls replied, then hung up.

34

Stone and Rocky were packing when one of Charter's men rapped on the door.

"Come in."

The man cracked the door. "I need the keys to the Porsche," he said. "We're going to drive it around the neighborhood for a few minutes, to try to suck in anybody who thinks he's following you."

Stone tossed him the key. "What are we riding in?"

"Our special van," the man replied. "After the Porsche is gone, we'll pull the van into the garage. You can board there."

Wilfred came for their luggage. "I'm nervous," Rocky said.

"That's unlike you. You're a field agent, you don't get nervous."

"Not so's you'd notice it, but I do."

"Let's go see what this vehicle of theirs is," Stone said.

"I hope it's not a garbage truck," Rocky replied.

They went down to the garage and found a Mercedes Sprinter waiting. It was dark blue and had the name J.P. ROCKINGHAM, POULTERER emblazoned on the side. When the door slid open, Stone found an interior much like a corporate jet: four facing seats and a table.

"I can stand this," Rocky said, sliding into a reclining chair.

The sliding door closed, and light filled the garage as the door opened.

"Now's the moment for an RPG," Rocky said.

"No, the opposition is out following the Porsche around."

They backed into the mews, and the garage door closed.

"What about the men in the pub?" Rocky asked.

"The pubs are closed this time of day," Stone replied. He handed her the *Times*. "Think about this, instead." He opened the *Guardian* to read himself.

The Sprinter made it out of the mews without being fired on, and soon they were mixed in with the westbound traffic, toward the M4.

"Everybody comfy back there?" The voice

came from a speaker above the table.

Stone pressed a button on it. "Just fine, thanks."

"No sign of a tail."

"Good news," Stone said, then went back to his paper.

Traffic was fairly heavy, but moving. Less than an hour later they turned off the motorway and drove for a few minutes to a large gate and through it without being stopped. Stone saw a sign reading ACE AIRCRAFT INTERIORS, and a minute later they turned into a parking lot and were let into a large hangar. Stone's G-500 was parked inside.

Charter opened the van door and let them out. "We're on schedule and tail free," he said. "The only moment I'm worried about is wheels up. That's when they could fire on the airplane from someplace out in a field off the airport."

"Thanks for mentioning that," Rocky said.

Rawls and Sally were waiting in their seats, drinking coffee.

"You do travel in style, Stone," Sally said.

"We do our best."

Charter, who'd been checking that everything was as it should be on board, came to bid Stone farewell. "I'm off," he said.

"Thanks for all your efforts to keep us

safe, Philip," Stone said, shaking his hand. Charter left the airplane, and the stewardess immediately closed and secured the door. A tractor began towing them out of the hangar. Once free and clear, Faith started the engines one by one. Apparently, all the checklists had been run in the hangar, because after a couple minutes of taxiing, the airplane turned onto the runway without stopping and accelerated.

Rocky closed her eyes. A moment later the airplane rotated, and the landing gear could be heard coming up. "Are we dead, yet?" she asked.

"We're free and clear," Stone said. "Next stop, Teterboro."

The stewardess came back to where they sat. "There's a call for you on the satphone," she said, handing it to him.

"Hello?"

"It's Mike," Freeman said. "I understand you're still alive."

"That's what they tell us. I'm looking forward to Teterboro, though."

"Only if we're sure it's viable," Mike said. "We've got people on the ground. If there's any doubt, we can divert to JFK or Newark."

"Whatever you say," Stone said.

"Talk to you later," Mike said, and hung up.

Stone picked up a two-day-old *New York Times* and looked for the crossword.

They were three hours into the flight when Stone got another satphone call.

"It's Philip," Charter said.

"Right."

"I want you to know, up front, that the next time you see the Porsche, the damage will have been repaired."

"Say again?"

"I'm afraid that the Greek's boys took our little feint a bit too seriously, and gunfire was exchanged."

"Were any of your people hurt?"

"No, just your car, and one more of the Greek's people is down."

"Well, at least we're outscoring them."

"I'm afraid that will just make him angrier."

"What was the damage?"

"As I said, when you see it again it will be perfect. That's all you need to know." Charter hung up.

"What was that about?" Rocky asked.

"Wrong number," Stone said, and started a new crossword.

■ ■ ■

Sometime later, the stewardess woke Stone from a deep nap. "We're twenty-five minutes out," she said.

"From which airport?"

"Teterboro. The coast is clear."

The plane touched down gently. When they made the turn for the hangar, Stone could see that the door was open. Just short of it, Faith cut the engines, and they were towed inside.

The aircraft door opened, and Mike Freeman came aboard. "Transportation awaits," he said, shaking Stone's hand. Stone introduced everybody, and when he could, he leaned close to Freeman's ear and whispered, "Don't mention the Porsche."

Mike nodded.

Fred was there with the Bentley, and there was one of Strategic Services' armored SUVs waiting for Ed and Sally. Forty minutes later, they all pulled into Stone's garage, and the door closed behind them.

"You can exhale now," he said to Rocky.

35

Stone walked into his office with Rocky trailing and, instead of Joan's sunny face, he was confronted by the mien of Lance Cabot, not so sunny.

"Welcome back, Stone. Rocky, we've missed you," Lance said.

Ed Rawls followed them in and took a seat.

Joan finally made an appearance. "Coffee, anyone? Snack?"

Everybody gave her a negative grunt or shook their heads.

"Then I'll leave you to the tender mercies of Mr. Cabot," she said, and disappeared into her office.

"How do you tolerate that woman, Stone?" Lance asked.

"Don't make me choose between you and Joan, Lance. You'd be dead in the water."

Lance took a deep breath and let out a noisy sigh. "We have to talk," he said. He

227

opened his briefcase, took out three iPhones — red, white, and a deep blue — set them on the coffee table, and slid each phone toward its intended recipient. "Red for you, Stone. White for you, Rocky. And blue for you, Ed. They all have the identical content to their predecessors, but they are each loaded with a new variation on the operating system and an all-new encryption system that we've been working on for a year. One that the Greek and his tech people couldn't penetrate even if they had a decade to work on it. I won't explain why, because you wouldn't understand it anyway. Just know that it works, and you can trust it. I'll have your old phones back, please."

Everybody slid their phones across the table toward him, then put away their new phones.

"Now," Lance said, as if to rivet their attention. "We have gone through two or three phases of this business with the Russians, and we're essentially down to two choices. The first is that we continue to kill as many of the Greek's people as we possibly can. He's already down five, and he seems to have an unlimited supply, but that can't be true. Also, we've lost one man, and we don't want to lose any more, especially one of you. The second choice is that we come to an accommodation with the Greek."

"Ha!" Stone said.

"I vote for both choices, simultaneously," Rawls said.

"I'm not voting," Rocky said.

"Your votes don't matter in the least," Lance said, "but your opinions may. Stone, any thoughts?"

"I'm too baffled to think. How the hell would we arrange for a meeting, just run up a white flag and ask them to trust us, while not trusting them?"

"That's close," Lance said. "I think the Greek would be intrigued enough to sit down and listen, at the very least."

"I think we should lure them into a meeting, then kill them all," Rawls said.

"Crude, but possibly effective," Lance said. "But word would eventually get out that we can't be trusted, and if you add that to the fact that hardly anybody trusts us, already, it could harm other efforts. Rocky?"

"My opinion," she said, "is that everything I've heard so far is crazy, and none of it would work."

"Perhaps you can come up with a different option," Lance said, as if he knew she couldn't.

"I like one where a lot of them end up dead, and none of us does. Although I haven't heard any details," she said, looking askance at Stone, "I think I liked the move in London, where Philip lured them into following the Porsche. They killed at least one, while losing no one, with the exception of some paint and glass off the Porsche."

"That puts you in Ed's camp, then," Lance said.

Rocky shook her head. "I'm not camping with Ed, though I'm sure he knows how to rub two weapons together and whip up a conflagration."

"I do," Ed replied, giving her a little salute. "Stone, let's hear from you."

"I miss Philip Charter," Stone said. "As you said, under his leadership, the score is the Greek five, us one. Apart from Ed's work as an assassin, which seemed to pour gasoline on the fire, Charter's approach seems to be the only thing that's working."

"I don't like losing even one to the Greek," Lance said.

"Who does? But maybe Philip can get the score down to zero for us, from here on."

"That's a ray of hope," Ed said, "and so far, the only one we've had."

Stone saw one of Lance's eyelids flutter a bit, and he took that to mean that he was extremely uncomfortable with the notion of bringing Philip Charter back onto the team.

"Lance, what are your objections to bringing Philip back to the lineup?"

Ed spoke up. "Asking Lance that is like asking the owner of the Patriots to bring back Tom Brady for more money."

That was apt enough to make Stone laugh, but he took care to laugh softly. It surprised him that Lance seemed to be actually considering the idea of Philip. That plan would have the virtue of having someone to blame if it all went wrong, and he guessed Lance would be attracted to that.

"All right," Lance said, confirming Stone's suspicion, "I'll ask Philip to rejoin our numbers."

"With full authority resting with Philip?" Rawls asked.

"Let's not go entirely mad," Lance said.

"It's the only way Philip takes all the blame if we come a cropper," Ed said. "Surely that's attractive."

"Also," Stone said, "Philip is not employed by the Agency, to the best of my knowledge, and even if he fails, he can go back to a very nice job at Strategic Services."

Lance saw a crack in the exit door, and he went for it. "All right," he said, "I'll phone Philip and make him an offer. If he accepts, we could have him here by tomorrow night. All of you just sit tight here and try to still

231

be alive when he arrives."

Without further ado, Lance rose and left the room, and the outside door to the street was heard opening and closing.

Joan stuck her head in. "He's gone. Anyone like coffee or a snack?"

"I'd like a drink," Rawls said.

"Then let's all get settled in and meet in the study at six for alcoholic beverages," Stone proposed.

His proposal was accepted.

"Joan, ask Helene to have dinner at seven for the four of us, and we'll be joined tomorrow evening by another stay-over guest."

"Right," Joan said. "Care to offer a name, rank, and gender?"

"Colonel Philip Charter, Royal Army, retired. Male. Alone, as far as I know."

"Will do," Joan said.

Stone directed Rawls to his room, where Sally was already waiting.

"Listen, Stone," Rawls said.

"I'm listening, Ed."

"We're going to need weapons and New York City licenses."

"I'll see what I can do," Stone said.

232

36

Upstairs, Stone closed the master suite door. Rocky was in her dressing room, unpacking.

"Rocky?"

"Speak."

"Can you persuade your Pod to loan us some weapons?"

She came out of the dressing room and sat on the bed. "What sort of firepower are we talking about, and for what purpose?"

"A handgun and a riot shotgun each — and ample ammo — for self-defense against those who would kill us."

"No hand grenades or automatic weapons?"

"We're in my house," Stone said. "I don't want to reduce it to rubble."

"I'll see what I can do."

Stone hung up his jacket and trousers, stretched out on his bed, and pressed the button that sat him up. He made a call.

"Bacchetti," Dino said.

"Hey, there. We're back in civilization again."

"About time. Anybody try to kill you today?"

"Only once — this morning. Somebody else was driving my car. No harm done, except to the car."

"Okay. You sound like you want something."

"I want to invite you and Viv to dinner tonight, here."

"We accept. What else?"

"You're such a cynic, Dino."

"No, I just know you too well."

"Well, I need two NYC carry licenses, one for Ed Rawls, whom you know. The other is for Dame Sarah Deerfield, recently retired chief of the London Metropolitan Police. They'll both be at dinner."

"I can do that, as long as nobody knows, and if I can have the licenses back when they're no longer needed by those parties. The licenses will also have thirty-day expiry dates."

"Agreed. Drinks at six, dinner at seven, just a jacket and tie will do."

"Okay."

"Bring the licenses."

"It sounds as though I should come

armed."

"It couldn't hurt. You and Viv both. Enter via the garage, and leave your vehicle there." Stone hung up, then called down to the kitchen to inform Helene of their new dinner count.

Rocky finished a call and hung up, too. "Done. The firearms will be delivered in half an hour. Let Joan know."

Stone made that call.

Dino showed up early, alone. "Viv is on the way," he said. "Now, tell me what the fuck is going on and why you're arming your guests."

Stone gave him the two-minute version and finished before Viv arrived. She gave Stone a kiss on the cheek. "First time I've been asked to come armed to dinner."

Dino gave her the one-minute version of events. "Where are the guns coming from?"

"They're in a case behind the door," Stone said. "Loaned by the New York station of the Agency."

"Does Lance know?"

"Lance knows everything."

"Or thinks he does," she said.

"He's usually right."

"I've heard about the Greek," Viv said. "Are you sure you have enough firepower?"

"Pretty much. I've got one of your people on the way to run things."

"Philip? Lance called me. He's our contribution. You don't have to pay him."

"Lance will be delighted to know that. Did he ask for house protection, too?"

"They're already in place, two inside, four outside."

"Bill Lance for those."

"Already done."

They had drinks in the study, then moved to the dining room.

"I've been thinking," Rawls said, "about this truce idea."

"What do you think?" Stone asked.

"I think it could work, if Lance puts enough threat behind it."

"Wouldn't that constitute bad faith on Lance's part?"

"Not if he gives them the opportunity to do the right thing. If they don't, they need to know that the worldwide reach of the Agency will be fully employed. At least, that's what Lance has to tell them. I honestly don't think he's up for that kind of fight."

"The threat should be enough," Stone said. "From what I've heard, the Greek is murderous, but not stupid. And he's already lost five men — seven if you count the Pentkovskys."

"Yeah, and it's not good for organizational morale if your coworkers are dropping like flies. The Greek can't maintain control if his worker bees are unhappy about the odds."

"Everything you've said is rational," Stone said, "unless the Greek isn't. If he pops his cork, then . . ."

"I don't want to think about that," Rawls said. "We have to have hope."

Sally spoke for the first time. "Hope is Philip Charter," she said. "Failure is unknown to him."

"I like the sound of that," Stone said.

37

Stone woke up the following morning and reached for Rocky. Instead, he found cold steel. He opened both eyes and located the two 12-gauge, short-barreled (18 1/2 inches) shotguns between them. After ascertaining that they were both on safety, he gingerly set them on the floor beside the bed.

"What are you doing?" Rocky asked, suddenly awake.

"Disarming you. You don't need two shotguns to handle me."

She snuggled closer. "I guess not."

"Did you put them in bed with us?"

"Last night. Didn't you notice?"

"Not until this morning, when I made my move — or tried to."

"I'm unarmed now," she said, feeling for him. "But you're not, and that's the way I like it."

They did what came naturally, then ordered breakfast.

Rocky took a bite of a breakfast sausage. "What time are you expecting Philip?"

"I haven't heard. Flights from London usually leave late morning or early afternoon, so I reckon he'll be here in time for drinks."

"I didn't order him any weapons."

"Let's deal with that after we've heard that he didn't bring any."

"If you say so."

"It's just a suggestion."

"I accept."

Stone's new red iPhone rang.

"Hello, Lance."

"How did you know it's not one of the others?"

"I always know when it's you. I get this queasy feeling."

"Nonsense. I hear you've armed yourself at our expense."

"We borrowed a few and will return them in due course."

"What about ammunition?"

"We'll return what we haven't fired at somebody."

"Well . . ."

"Lance, why did you call? Do you remember?"

"Of course, I remember."

"Would you like to share it with me?"

"I just wondered what time Philip is arriving."

"I don't know. He hasn't shared that with me."

"Is he coming armed?"

"Once again, I don't know."

"Oh."

"Lance, I have to shower and dress now. Is there anything else? Anything at all?"

"Watch yourself. The Greek is tricky."

"That's excellent advice. Goodbye." Stone hung up.

"I take it that was Lance."

"Yes, and he's very nervous. He couldn't even remember why he called."

"That makes *me* nervous," she said. "What does he know that we don't know?"

"If there's anything, he didn't share it."

Philip Charter, the perfect houseguest, arrived just in time to change for dinner and join them for cocktails. Stone introduced Dino and Viv. They imbibed, dined, and repaired to the study for cognac and coffee.

Finally, Philip cleared his throat. "Lance didn't tell me much," he said.

"He didn't tell us *anything,*" Stone replied. "What did he tell you?"

"He has an idea that we should declare a truce with the Greek, and see if we can negotiate a more permanent peace."

"He mentioned that," Stone said, "but we don't know how to establish contact with the Greek, and Lance didn't share that information."

"Ed, I'm told that your plan is to kill anybody who shows up to discuss peace," Philip said.

"It's all I could come up with, Philip. We were sort of hoping that you'd have some ideas about how we should conduct ourselves."

"Lance doesn't want us to do that. He says if word got around it would ruin the Agency's reputation for trustworthiness."

"I wasn't aware that the Agency had a reputation for trustworthiness," Ed replied.

Philip took a slow sip of his brandy and swirled it around his mouth. "I think I can get a message to the Greek about the idea of a truce."

"Suppose he takes us up on it?" Stone asked. "What would your next move be?"

"To find a mutually acceptable venue for our talks and agree on some ground rules."

"Do you have a venue in mind?"

"I'm off my turf," Philip said. "Do you have any ideas?"

"What would we require of a venue?"

"Something like a conference room," Philip replied, "with at least two escape routes, in case things don't work out."

"Maybe at a hotel?" Stone suggested.

"All right."

"There's an elegant small hotel called the Crane, uptown a few blocks. It has a conference room. It's separated from the lobby by a tinted glass wall."

"How dark is the tinting?"

"Not too dark. You can see who's in the lobby."

"What about egress?"

"There's a door that leads to the kitchen," Stone said. "In case you want lunch or coffee."

"What happens when you get to the kitchen?"

"I've never been to the kitchen, but kitchens always have access to the street, for food deliveries, laundry, et cetera."

"I'll get Mike Freeman to send somebody there to case the place and draw us a floor plan," Philip said.

"I can handle that," Viv said. "No need to bother Mike."

"All right, Viv. Tomorrow morning, perhaps?"

"That should be all right."

"How many people from each side?" Rawls asked.

"I'd suggest two for our side."

"You'll need a third man from each side to frisk the participants. We don't want a shootout, if there's a difference of opinion."

"I'll be happy to frisk for our team," Rocky said.

"Have you dealt with Russians before, Rocky?" Philip asked.

"Only across a table."

"I'm not sure the Russian ego is equipped to be frisked by a woman, no reflection on you. Their opinion of women seems to be — how can I put this delicately? — antediluvian."

Rocky laughed. "Point made and taken."

"That leaves you, Dino."

"I think I can handle that," Dino said drily.

Rawls spoke up. "I'll establish myself outside the kitchen door."

"For what purpose?" Philip asked.

"To shoot anybody who comes out after shots have been fired inside."

"Good thinking," Philip said. "Now, I need to get some sleep to dispel the jet lag. I'll send a message out, and perhaps it will reach the Greek tomorrow morning."

They adjourned, and Stone felt better that a plan was, at last, forming.

Philip excused himself and went to his room.

"Anybody feeling better about this?" Stone asked, when Philip had gone.

Nobody spoke. Everybody looked glum.

38

The following morning, Philip Charter called his London office and asked for his assistant, Ashley Parks.

"Ashley Parks."

"Good morning, it's Philip."

"Good morning, Colonel," she replied in her plummy, girls-school accent.

"Please call me Philip," he said. He had been trying to get her to do that since he had hired her, some weeks before, in the hope that doing so might warm the atmosphere between them.

So far, it had not worked. "Yes, sir," she replied.

"I want you to find someone in the office who has contacts inside the London underworld and see if that person can communicate with a man known as the Greek, who is, apparently, head of the Russian Mob."

"I shall do so at once. What is the message?"

"To call me on my cell phone for a brief chat that would benefit both of us. I would be grateful if he could communicate by seven PM, London time. Tell him there will be no one else on the call, just the two of us. And it will take no longer than two minutes."

"Got it," Ashley replied, scribbling on her steno pad. "Will there be anything else, Colonel?"

"Yes, please. Henceforth, call me Philip and don't make me have to remind you again." He hung up.

Philip ordered up breakfast and it was delivered in record time. By the time he had finished, his phone was ringing.

"This is Philip Charter."

"You requested a chat wif somebody," a Cockney-accented voice said.

"That is correct."

"Why ever would you want that?"

"I would like to discuss the possibility of a truce between his people and mine."

The man hung up, and Philip was left staring at his phone. He was about to step into his shower when the phone rang again. "This is Philip Charter."

"This is the person you asked to speak

246

to," a voice said.

"Good, Mr. . . ."

"Smith," the man said.

"Very well. I believe it would be to your benefit, and mine, if you and I could meet and discuss the matter of a truce between us."

There was a deep chuckle from the other end. "You think you can just snap your fingers, and we're friends?"

"I believe that reasonable men can come to terms, if there is a modicum of goodwill between them, and if it is to the benefit of them both."

"How much goodwill are we talking about?"

"I'm not talking about money, just the cessation of violence."

"For how long?"

"Permanently, if neither party breaks the truce with violence."

"Why would I deal with somebody who has killed five of my people?"

"I would like to point out the fact that four of these people were killed in a traffic accident while they were trying to kill either me or my client or both. Also, my client had nothing to do with the demise of the first two victims. He did not know them and, he believes, they did not know him."

"Who is your client?"

"An American gentleman called Stone Barrington."

"I heard the name, once."

"Are you willing to meet at a place agreed to by all parties?"

"Where?"

"Mr. Barrington and I are both in New York."

"What a coincidence! So am I! Where do you want to meet?"

"There is a hotel on Madison Avenue called the Crane."

"I know it."

"There is a conference room off the main lobby that would be suitable for us. Why don't you send someone over there to inspect the property and see if it is sufficient to your needs?"

"How did you happen to choose this place?"

"I described to Mr. Barrington the sort of place that would be acceptable to me, and he suggested the Crane. I believe he had a drink or dinner there once and was favorably impressed." Philip had no idea if this was true, but it couldn't hurt.

"I'll get back to you later today," Smith said, then hung up.

Philip called Stone. "We've got a bite from

the Greek," he said.

"How good a bite?"

"A solid tug on the line. He's thinking about it. So far, he hasn't objected to the venue, either. By the way, how did you come up with the Crane?"

"I passed by there once, was intrigued, and walked through the bar and the restaurant."

"How long ago?"

"Perhaps a month. I believe it has only recently opened. So you think he's going to go for it?"

"He sounded interested."

"What's his last name?"

"He wants to be called Smith. Oh, by the way, he says he's in New York."

"Probably came here to kill me," Stone said.

"That's not out of the question. I assured him that you had nothing to do with any of the killings of his people."

"Well, we'd better not let him get a look at Ed Rawls. He might be a familiar face to them."

"I'll keep that in mind," Charter said. "He said he'd get back to me today."

"Keep me posted." They hung up.

Stone's phone rang. "Yes?"

"It's Joan. Your motorcycle has just been delivered. I had them put it in the garage. It's gorgeous, by the way."

"Thank you, I'm delighted to hear it." He hung up and turned to Rocky. "You want to see something beautiful?"

"You don't need an excuse to take off your pants," she said.

"Not that, thank you. Come with me." He took her down to the garage and pulled the cover off the bike.

"Ooooh!" she said. "A '51 Norton!"

"How did you know that?" he asked, impressed.

"I looked at one in a showroom on Third Avenue once," she said. "I couldn't afford it."

"This is the same bike. I'm afraid I had a little accident on my first ride. It just came back from the shop."

"Can we ride it?"

"I'm afraid we're confined to quarters at the moment."

"That's right," she said. "I forgot."

"Have you ever driven a Norton?"

"I used to have a boyfriend who had one, but nowhere as nice as this one."

"We'll get around to it," Stone said. "When we've taken care of this other thing."

"Any news on that?"

"Philip's got a nibble."

39

Philip Charter got out of a taxi a few doors down from the Crane and walked slowly up the opposite side of the street. The hotel had a sleek, black marble front, chiseled with a gilt-filled line drawing of a bird, standing on one leg. There was no name on the building.

Carrying a briefcase, so as to appear to be a businessman, he crossed at the corner and walked briskly toward the hotel, looking at the other side of the street, particularly for a good spot to locate a sniper. He had no intention of doing that, but he thought it might occur to the Greek. There was a fancy delicatessen there, with three floors above, which could be offices or apartments. There was also a roof that could make a good perch, but there was no window between where the conference room was located, so anyone getting shot would have to be entering or leaving through a set of front doors, which were smoked glass. He concluded that a sniper would not be a factor.

He entered the Crane through the revolving door, stopped, and looked around. The front desk was dead ahead, the bar and restaurant were to his right, and the conference room was where it was supposed to be, on his left.

He walked into the bar, set his briefcase on a stool, and sat down beside it.

A bartender approached. "May I serve you something, sir?"

"Thanks, I'm meeting a friend. I'll wait until he arrives." The bartender left him alone. He could see through the smoked glass into the lobby, which indicated that he would have much the same view from the conference room. He made a show of looking at his watch a couple of times, then he picked up his briefcase and left, walking downtown, toward Stone's house. As he walked he got out his phone and called Dino Bacchetti.

"Commissioner's office," a man said.

"Colonel Philip Charter, for Commissioner Bacchetti."

"Bacchetti."

"Dino, it's Philip."

"What can I do for you, Philip?"

"Can you tell me where in the city departments I can find an architect's plan of the ground floor of the Crane Hotel?"

Dino didn't hesitate. "I won't punish you by giving you directions. I'll send somebody to pick it up and bring it with me to dinner tonight."

"Wonderful, thank you."

"You're welcome." Dino hung up.

He was back at the house in Stone's office with Stone and Rocky when Joan came into the room. "A Mr. Smith is on the phone for you, Colonel."

Stone pointed to the handset on the coffee table, and Philip picked it up. "This is Colonel Charter."

"This is Smith," the man said. His voice was a little gravelly, with an indeterminate accent. "The Crane is okay with us. Conditions are: Barrington and a companion, with me and one of my people. Everybody gets frisked in the lobby, and I mean *frisked.* Three PM tomorrow."

"Those are acceptable conditions. We'll want our own frisker there, too. I also need a phone number on which to contact you, should there be any changes in the plan. You already have mine." Smith gave him a New York City cell number, then hung up.

Stone had been listening on his extension.

254

"So, we're on. Was that too easy?"

"I don't think we can complain about that," Charter replied. "And his conditions are the same as ours. I had a look at the place a while ago, and it works for me." He turned to Rocky. "Can you check if the Agency has recovered any of their files on the Greek?"

"Sure," Rocky said. She left the room for a few minutes, then came back "We can't have the file, but a summary is being e-mailed to us on Stone's phone."

Stone got into his desktop e-mail program and waited for it to pop up. It took only a few minutes, then Stone printed out copies for each of them.

It was only one page, plus a poor photograph of a man who appeared to be short and stocky. "He looks a little like Aristotle Onassis," he said.

"Maybe that's how he got his sobriquet," Philip suggested. "Let's see. Serge Anatolovich Gromyko. Born in Chechnya fifty-one years ago. Served in the Soviet Army, then deserted to fight in the Chechen rebellion, got a name for killing readily and viciously."

"That's it, I guess," Stone said, reading through the document.

"There's something else you could do,

255

Rocky," Philip said.

"Yes?"

"Tomorrow, see if you can spot him entering the hotel, then follow him when he leaves the Crane and see where he goes. Can you do that without getting yourself killed?"

"I believe so."

"Don't take any risks," Stone said. "If we lose him, it won't be a disaster."

"I'll have a man on the roof across the street," Philip said. "If there's any shooting inside, he will take out Mr. Gromyko as he leaves."

"I think Ed would enjoy that," Stone said.

"Good idea. Rocky, can you get him a sniper's rifle that will fit into a briefcase?"

"Probably. I think one of your people should watch Ed's back. Gromyko might be a step ahead of us."

"I don't like to think about that," Philip said.

"Nevertheless, we should think about it."

Joan came back into Stone's office. "Lance Cabot is on line one, and he wants to speak to all of you."

Stone pressed the speaker button. "Lance?"

"Indeed. Are you all there?"

"Rawls is not."

"That's all right. He wouldn't listen to me anyway."

"Listen to you about what?" Stone asked.

"We must be cautious about this meeting with the Greek, who we now know as Comrade Gromyko. By the way, he's no relation to the late Soviet foreign minister."

"Good to know," Stone said, drily.

"He is, however, just as slippery and just as untrustworthy."

"Oh?"

"I fear it was a mistake to allow him to choose the venue."

"Lance," Stone said, "I am surprised that one as well-informed as you does not know that *I* first suggested the Crane, for no other reason than I thought it was what we needed."

"You were not aware, then, that Gromyko *owns* the Crane?"

"You're kidding."

"I kid you not. Oh, there are a couple of corporate names between him and owner-ship, but he owns the links, too."

"Lance," Philip said. "My primary worry in all this was getting the Greek to accept a meeting place that we could deal with. Even if this monumental coincidence is true, we have achieved this purpose, and he doesn't know that we know that he owns the place."

"I should think that he believes that you do," Lance said.

"And how is that to our disadvantage? If he wanted to kill us, he wouldn't do it in midtown Manhattan, in a hotel that he owns."

Lance paused. "Point taken. All right, we just have to be careful, and try not to kill or capture the Greek on his turf."

"We can do that," Philip replied. Everybody hung up.

"I don't know how he does that," Stone said. "I've had this office swept a dozen times, and we've never found a bug."

258

40

Ed Rawls came back from wherever he'd been and joined them in Stone's office. "Anything new?"

"We're on for three o'clock tomorrow at the Crane," Stone replied.

"Well, that suits me to a T," Ed said.

"I'm not sure I like the sound of that," Stone said. "What do you have in mind?"

"Possibilities, Stone, only possibilities."

"Do any of those possibilities have anything to do with killing the Greek?"

"Possibly," Rawls replied. "But they are only if-then ideas."

"As in . . . ?"

"As in: If the Greek kills one or all of you, then should I kill the Greek?"

"Most assuredly," Philip replied. "I shouldn't like to have him get away with such a horror."

"I don't think even Lance could object to that," Stone said.

"Well, then . . ."

"Well, those are the only circumstances I can think of that would give you such largesse to dispense."

"I'm a generous guy," Rawls said.

"Not tomorrow, you're not. If you're really contemplating that, I'll leave an 'in case of my death' note with Dino, telling him you did it and to arrest you at once."

"That's an extreme tactic, Stone, and not worthy of you."

"Nevertheless. I want your word that you will not make any attempt on the Greek while any one of us is still alive."

"Oh, all right. You've got it."

"When was the last time you gave your word to somebody, Ed?" Stone asked.

"Almost never."

"So this is a new experience for you."

"Pretty much."

"All right, I'll accept your word. But if you break your promise, I'll never trust you again about anything."

"Fair enough."

"Something else for you to consider, Ed," Philip said.

"What's that?"

"If you appear on a rooftop or in any window overlooking the hotel with the sniper's weapon Rocky is about to give you,

260

you will almost certainly be looking down the barrel of *their* sniper's rifle."

Ed swallowed hard. "I hadn't yet got to the point of thinking about that, but I would have, eventually."

Everybody had a good laugh.

"Now that we've got that out of the way," Rocky said, setting a briefcase on the coffee table, "I have this for you."

Ed opened the briefcase and laughed aloud.

"We believe it's Czech, but we don't know for sure."

"Stone," Ed said, "do you have a magnifying glass?"

Stone produced one from a desk drawer.

Ed removed the major part of the rifle from its case and removed the bolt, then he put the barrel under Stone's desk lamp and held the glass under it. "What do you see there?" he asked.

Everybody crowded around and had a look.

"I see the letters *e* and *r,*" Rocky said.

"Those are my initials. I built this weapon and another just like it. I still have one, and I always wondered what had happened to the other. Now I know the Agency stole it."

"More likely," Rocky said, "you stole the other one from the Agency."

261

The group wandered off to dress for dinner, but Rocky stayed in Stone's office. "Something I want from you," she said.

"I can't think of anything I wouldn't give you," Stone offered.

"I want the Norton."

"Except that."

"Not forever, just for tomorrow afternoon."

"What do you propose to do with it?"

"To follow you and Lance when you leave the Crane, to ensure no trouble follows you. In Manhattan traffic, following in a car would be very difficult; on the Norton, much easier."

"What is your experience with driving Nortons?" Stone asked.

"You first."

"Okay, just the once."

"And it needed considerable repair after that?"

"Well, yes."

"I drove my boyfriend's Norton a couple of dozen times, in city and country, and never put a scratch on it."

"Since you appear to be the more qualified driver, you may use the Norton for the stated purpose. Do you have the proper clothing?"

"Yes, it's the only thing left of that relationship. I'll have to run by my apartment to pick it up, though."

"Get Fred to drive you there and bring you back. And go armed."

"I had intended to," she said.

41

Dino and Viv arrived for dinner, Dino with a cardboard tube under his arm. "I've got the plan for the ground floor of the Crane," he said to Philip.

They spread it out on the coffee table and had a look.

"It is as I had imagined it," Philip said.

"As you can see," Dino said, pointing, "the door to the kitchen leads to a hallway, and there is an elevator at the end of the hall. I think you should let me put a man there, in case the Greek calls for reinforcements to arrive from an upper floor."

"An excellent idea," Philip said. "I didn't know about the elevator. How many floors does it reach?"

"All the way to the top, I expect. They're not going to stop delivering room service orders halfway up."

"Good point. We'll need a man to frisk the Greek and his colleague outside the conference room."

"I thought I'd handle that, myself," Dino replied.

"Suppose they recognize you?"

"Then they'll be impressed that you could deploy the police commissioner to handle a mundane task."

"Be sure that no one is carrying a knife, as well as a gun."

"That goes without saying. Cops don't stop when they find one weapon. They get dead that way."

"I suggest that you deploy two detectives, a man and a woman, both armed, in the bar across the lobby. The door to the conference room is visible through a glass wall from there, and we haven't promised not to put armed people there."

"Okay. Their first job will be to spot the people that the Greeks have stationed in the bar."

"Ah, yes."

"And, if the Greek tries to leave the building out the rear hallway and kitchen, have your man in the back hall radio that to us. We want to follow them."

"Done."

"And you're going to have a man to watch Rawls's back on the opposite roof, too?"

"Yes."

"Good. I don't have any more questions. Stone?"

"That covers it for me, but I'd like to know who the Greek is bringing with him."

"I'll ask."

Dino spoke up. "I'll run his guy through the system to see who we're dealing with."

Dino put away his map, and they went into the study for drinks.

Lance called.

"Yes, Lance?" Stone said.

"Have you run through your task for tomorrow?"

"We just finished."

"Did you forget anything?"

"If we had forgotten something we wouldn't know it, would we?"

"Are you ready for any eventuality?"

"Any eventuality we could think of. Perhaps you should have made the trip to New York to inspect our plan."

"I'm at the Carlyle; invite me to dinner."

"Lance, we'd be delighted if you would join us for dinner. Drinks now, dinner at seven-thirty."

"I'm nearly there," Lance said. "May I enter through the garage?"

"Of course. Ring once when you're here, then hang up and I'll open the door."

Stone hung up, and his phone immediately

rang once, then stopped. Stone pressed the button on his iPhone, then called Helene and told her to add a place for dinner.

Lance entered the room alone, then said, "I hope it's all right that I brought another guest."

"Of course, who . . ."

"Ladies and gentlemen, the President of the United States."

Holly Barker strode in, looking fabulous, and greeted everyone, stopping at Rocky.

"And who might this be?"

"I'm sorry, Madam President," Lance said. "I am remiss. This is Ms. Roxanne Hardwick of the Agency's New York station. She's known to everyone as Rocky."

The two women shook hands, sizing up each other. "An honor, Madam President," Rocky said.

"And a pleasure," Holly replied, firing a glance at Stone. "Let's all use 'Holly,' shall we? To make me feel more at home?"

Stone poured her a vodka gimlet, and Lance a single malt Scotch, and they found seats, then he called Helene and added yet another guest at dinner.

"Well," Holly said, "is the planning all done for the demise of the Greek?"

"Ah," Lance said, "you may recall that we gave up the notion of his demise at an earlier meeting. This one is strictly a peace conference, unless they commit the poor judgment of starting something."

"Well, yes," Holly replied, "there's always the possibility of that, when dealing with such people, isn't there? And you are prepared for that possibility?"

"We are, to the extent that is possible to do so," Lance said.

"I met the Greek once," Holly said.

The group fell into silence.

"Really?" Lance finally managed. "Where and under what circumstances?"

"In Greece," she replied. "I attended a dinner party hosted by a Greek shipping magnate named Stavros something-or-other, in the company of Aristotle Onassis." No one interrupted her, so she continued, "I was there for security reasons. My superiors were uncomfortable with the idea of Onassis being in the same room as someone who held the reputation of the Greek for an entire evening."

"What were your impressions of the Greek?" Stone asked.

"He made a considerable effort to remain cool in the presence of the great man, but failed. I expect that part of his failure was wearing the same suit as Onassis's and from the same tailor."

"And how did Onassis react to that?"

"He seemed amused at the first moment they met, then not. Later I heard an office rumor that Onassis had changed his tailor, and that the name of the new one was held closely by his staff."

"Was any business discussed?" Philip asked.

"Only braggadocio about the tonnage of their fleets. Onassis never rose to the bait. I suspect he was a good poker player."

"How did the evening end?" Stone asked.

"I was dropped off at my hotel, after declining an invitation to stay the night aboard Onassis's yacht."

"That must have been a first for Onassis," Lance said quietly, getting a laugh from the group.

Holly smiled. "I was flattered, professionally, by his surprise."

"What did the Greek call himself on that occasion?"

"He called himself Gromyko, his own name. I expect he knew that Onassis, if he chose, could learn who he was, and he didn't want to be caught in a lie."

"Anything else?" Stone asked.

"Gromyko had impeccable table manners, but was awkward enough to make me think he had been trained by an expert just for the occasion."

"That's an astute observation," Lance said.

Then Fred announced dinner, and they made their way to the dining room, where Joan had thoughtfully placed Holly at the head of the table, with Philip and Lance to her left and right. Stone was at the other end, bracketed by Viv and Rocky.

Stone raised his glass and said, "Bon appétit," and dinner began.

42

They were on port and Stilton when, from the study, came the muffled but discernible sound of a cell phone.

"Excuse me," Holly said, rising, "I believe that's mine." Everyone rose with her, and she waved them down. "I won't be a moment." She went into the study and closed the door behind her.

"I hope this isn't about our little foray tomorrow," Lance said.

Holly came back into the room and sat down. After everyone had been reseated she said, "That call was about tomorrow afternoon's meeting at the Crane."

"What news?" Lance asked.

"Gromyko's colleague at the meeting will be named Pentkovsky."

Dead silence ensued.

"Relax," she said, "not *that* Pentkovsky, nor the other one, either. This one is called Egon, the youngest of three brothers."

"He is no less unwelcome," Lance said. "The other two brothers' reputations were as assassins."

"This one is said to be an accountant, one his colleagues call 'The Greek's Brain.' " Holly looked around the table. "Does this change your plan?"

"I'll be across the street," Rawls said, "so it doesn't change mine."

"Lance," Stone said, "why have we never heard of this third brother?"

"The president's sources are better than mine," Lance replied.

"Ah," Stone said.

"I don't see why this news should cause us any great concern," Lance said. "Some concern, perhaps, but not great concern."

Several cell phones went off, nearly simultaneously, and their owners dug them out.

Stone looked a photograph that he had just received. He held it up for the table to see, and everyone else held up their phones; they all had the same photograph. It was of a young man, perhaps early thirties, handsome and wearing a sharply tailored business suit.

"The president's sources are to be complimented," Lance said.

"And her telephone operators," Stone added. "Anyone recognize him?"

"He looks like a Pentkovsky," Rawls said, "but I've never seen him."

"Nor have I," Lance said. "Anybody?"

Heads were shaken.

"Dino," Stone said. "I suggest you pay particular attention to frisking him tomorrow."

"Duly noted," Dino replied.

"Then our meet tomorrow will proceed as planned," Lance said. "Unless anyone can give me a good reason why it shouldn't."

Heads were shaken.

"Well," Stone said. "If we're agreed, I suggest we adjourn to the living room for cognac and coffee."

They trailed into the room next door and everyone waited for Holly to choose a seat before distributing themselves about the room and sitting down.

"Would you like us to walk you through tomorrow's plan, Holly?" Lance asked.

"I think not," she said. "I would be too nervous if what actually happens deviates from the plan."

"Something usually happens," Lance said. "The Prussian general Helmuth von Moltke the Elder once said that 'No battle plan ever survives contact with the enemy.'"

"That's comforting, Lance," Stone said.

"It's the sort of advice that keeps one on

one's toes," Lance replied, somewhat smugly.

"And makes presidents nervous," Holly said. Her phone rang once again, and this time it was within reach. She answered it and pressed a button. "I think I'd better take this one in the car, on the way to the Carlyle. Lance, are you coming?"

"Yes, ma'am," Lance said, and they both said their good nights. Stone escorted them to their car, then returned to the living room.

"Well," Rocky said, "that was interesting."

It occurred to Stone that she was unaware of his continuing relationship with Holly Barker. "Yes, it was. It's good to know that our president takes an interest in what we're doing."

"Yeah," Dino said, "but officially she knows nothing about it."

"Sometimes it's best if it's that way," Stone said.

Dino got out his phone and gazed at the photo of Egon Pentkovsky. "He looks so innocent," he said.

"You don't believe he's just an accountant, do you?" Ed Rawls asked. "The two guys in the plumber's truck looked innocent, too, until they thought about shooting at me."

Stone grimaced. "Ed, let's not."

274

Rawls looked at the faces around the room and realized he had put his foot in it. "Aw, shit," he said.

"Maybe you should tell us about the plumber's truck, Ed," Rocky said.

"You don't want to know."

"I already know about the truck. Now I need to know what happened in it and how it affects tomorrow."

Stone tried to intervene. "I think we need to keep that on a need-to-know basis, Ed."

"I just said I need to know," Rocky replied.

"No, you *want* to know, and that's a different thing," Stone said.

"Maybe when I'm dead and gone," Rawls said. "Come to think of it, that may be tomorrow night. Can you wait that long?"

"Oh, all right," Rocky said, "but remember, I'm providing the weapons for this gig, and I need to know how they're going to be used."

"I think that remains to be seen," Stone said. "Remember, we're going in without weapons."

"I haven't made any promises along those lines," Rocky replied. "But then, I won't be inside, unless I hear weapons fire."

"On that note," Stone said, "I'm sending you all to bed. We need a good night's sleep."

"We'll see about that," Rocky whispered as she brushed past him.

"We'll have a light lunch tomorrow about eleven-thirty," Stone said, then followed Rocky to bed. When he got there, she was already in it, looking fetching.

"You know what I like about you?" Stone asked.

"What?"

"Absolutely everything — so far." He was shortly in the game.

43

Everybody had a sandwich and some soup. Lance arrived in time for that.

"What, no president?" Stone asked.

"She knows what she wants to know, now. She seems confident in us."

"I hope her confidence is not misplaced," Stone said. Rawls left first, since he had preparations to make. Rocky, dressed in black leather, rode the Norton out of the garage and out of sight. Stone, Lance, and Dino got into a black SUV, provided by Lance, and drove the few blocks uptown, waiting a block away from the Crane. At one minute to three they drove the last block, got out at the front door, and went inside, making a point of not looking anywhere but at the door to the conference room.

As the front door closed behind them, two men in dark suits walked in and past them to the conference room door, where they waited. The older one did, indeed, resemble Aristotle Onassis, and the younger one resembled the photo in everyone's iPhone. The older one stuck out his hand to Stone, who was the tallest of the group. "I am Gromyko," he said.

Stone shook the hand and looked him in the eye. "I am Barrington," he replied. "Good morning. My companions are Mr. Cabot, who will join me in our meeting, and Mr. Bacchetti, who will search both of you for weapons."

"Good," Gromyko said. "And my man behind you will search you." He raised his hands to shoulder level. Everyone underwent a thorough grope fest, then the Greek opened the door and led the way into the room.

To Stone's surprise, the man did not take a seat but, instead, walked around the conference table and through the door leading to the kitchen. Stone looked back and saw Dino and Gromyko's man eyeing each other suspiciously, then he followed the Greek through the door and into the back hall. The door closed behind him.

At the end of the hall another of Gromyko's men stood, holding open an elevator door.

"Please," Gromyko said holding out an

ushering hand.

Stone wasn't sure why, but he got on the elevator, which comfortably held them all. The car began to rise and continued for longer than Stone had expected. Lance was behind him, so they couldn't make eye contact.

The elevator door slid silently open, and they stepped into a large living room, at the center of which was a glass coffee table with four Charles Eames lounge chairs arranged around it. They took seats, and Stone ended up next to Gromyko.

A man in a white waiter's jacket emerged from what must have been the kitchen and approached the table. "Good day, gentlemen," he said. "May I offer you coffee, tea, sandwiches, or anything else?"

Gromyko indicated that Stone should order first. "A double espresso," he said. Might as well stay awake.

The others ordered something, and Gromyko waited until everyone had been served, then said, "Why are we here?" he asked.

"I would like to propose that we end hostilities," Lance said.

"What's in that for me?" the Greek asked.

"Staying alive," Stone said, "as it is for each of us."

279

Gromyko laughed, to Stone's relief. "Let us say that we agree in principle, depending on how our further discussions go."

"What further discussions are those?" Lance asked.

"Let us first discuss the disposition of two men in a plumber's van," the Greek said.

"You mean the two heavily armed assassins who were firing at an acquaintance of mine? They were disposed of."

"How may I find their remains?"

"I would advise conducting a search of the bottom of Penobscot Bay," Stone replied.

Gromyko frowned. "The men had families."

"The men chose risky careers. I'm sure their employer will take good care of their survivors."

"Where is the man, Rawls?"

"He was not invited to this meeting," Lance said. "It's difficult to know where he is at any given moment, as I'm sure you have learned."

"I have lost two brothers," the younger Pentkovsky, Egon, cut in.

"Our condolences," Stone replied. "I expect they understood the nature of their work, and its hazards."

"I expect their families to be compensated

280

for their loss," Pentkovsky said.

"That is entirely up to you," Lance said.

"You are being difficult," Gromyko said.

"I am being honest with you."

"You lack diplomacy."

Lance smiled. "As do you."

"I should think that a representative of the government of the United States should be authorized to offer compensation."

"I represent only a small department of the government of the United States, and all our expenditures are overseen by various committees of the Congress. You may, of course, bring suit against the government for this compensation, but that would certainly entail more scrutiny of your business and personal affairs than you are accustomed to."

"Surely you understand that I do not expect to leave this meeting empty-handed."

"I am surprised that you have any expectations at all in that regard," Lance said.

"It is a matter of respect," Gromyko said.

"Respect must be earned," Lance said.

"On the other hand," Stone said, "we do not intend any disrespect. All we seek is, as we said at the outset, a cessation of hostilities, which surely would have rewards for all of us."

"But you are unwilling to pay for it."

"For that or anything else," Lance said "Not even the coffee."

"That is not courteous," Gromyko said.

"Neither was the abrupt change of our agreed venue," Stone replied. "How many weapons are concealed near where you sit?"

Gromyko grimaced.

"Excuse me," Egon Pentkovsky said. "My associate does not deal so much with our legitimate business affairs. He is more accustomed to dealing with people who are, shall we say, less refined."

"I'm happy to know that some of your affairs are legitimate," Stone said. "Perhaps that should make this meeting easier for all of us."

"Serge said, at the outset, that we agree in principle with ending hostilities. Perhaps we can consider that a given and proceed with business matters."

Lance spoke up. "We are not aware that there is any business between us."

"I believe, Mr. Cabot, that your department of your government, the CIA, sometimes comes into possession of goods that are of no use to the Agency. Perhaps we could ease their reintroduction to markets and give your Agency significant funds, which could be applied to its various projects."

"I'm afraid that my Agency does not do business of the sort you suggest. We are not a profit-making organization; we seek only knowledge of our adversaries."

"We are disappointed," Egon said.

"I am sorry for your disappointment," Lance said. "Do we have agreement on the cessation of hostilities?"

Egon looked at Serge, who seemed to nod slightly. "We are agreed," Egon said.

"With immediate effect, we presume?" Another tiny nod.

"Good. I think we should all believe that this has been a successful discussion." Lance stood.

Stone stood with him, then, reluctantly, Gromyko and Pentkovsky stood as well. The waiter materialized and pressed the button for the elevator. Gromyko waved them in first, then followed.

No word was spoken as they traveled down.

Stone tensed slightly as the car slowed to a stop, half expecting men with machine guns to greet them as they got out.

The four men exchanged handshakes in the conference room, then Stone and Lance walked out the front door into brilliant sunshine. Stone resisted the urge to search the rooftop for Rawls, then got into the waiting SUV. Dino was in his own vehicle and preceded them to Stone's house.

No one died.

44

Ed Rawls tensed as Stone and Lance left the Cranc and got into the SUV. He sat back and surveyed every inch of the rooftop across the street, every window in view. Nothing, just Rocky following their SUV on the Norton as they departed.

He packed up and made his way downstairs to the street and took a taxi to Stone's house. He found Stone and his guests sharing a bottle of champagne in Stone's study.

"Come in, Ed," Stone said, "and have a glass." He nodded toward the bar, where an ice bucket and flutes awaited and watched as Rawls poured himself one. He took a stool and surveyed the happy group.

"You all look very pleased with yourselves," he said. "Did you get to kill anybody?"

"It all went smoothly," Stone said. "We have a truce."

"When pigs do aerial somersaults in the

sky," Ed replied.

"It was all very cordial," Lance said, "except the parts where they tried to extort money from us for the widows, if such exist, of the two men you dealt with in Maine. Gromyko seemed to want his plumber's van back. Stone referred him to the depths of Penobscot Bay."

"I'll give it twenty-four hours before they're up to mischief again," Rawls said.

"Just what do you mean by 'mischief'?" Lance asked.

"Murder and mayhem."

"I don't think we'll have any of that," Lance said.

"Why? Did you appeal to their sense of honor? They don't know what that is."

"We appealed to their sense of self-preservation," Stone said. "They have one of those."

"Well, while you're waiting for them to figure that out, my suggestion is that you maintain the same level of security that you have for the past few days."

"It couldn't hurt," Dino said.

"I'm agreeable to that," Lance added. "It's the prudent thing to do. And while we're at it, don't you hunt any of them down, Ed."

"I can restrain myself," Rawls said, "until they start shooting again. I don't think I'll go back to Maine for a while, maybe not until the snow falls."

"Do you still have your house in Virginia, Ed?" Lance asked. "A very pretty place."

"I do, and they won't know about it."

"Well, when I fly south, in a day or two, I'm happy to give you a chopper ride. After all, it's quite close to Langley."

"That's a kind offer, Lance. I'll consider it after discussing it with Sally."

She beamed at him over her champagne flute.

"I assume they took you to another part of the hotel after you entered the conference room," Rawls said to Stone.

"Yes. They took us up to a penthouse and gave us coffee."

"You're lucky you're not floating facedown in the East River," he said.

Ed looked out over the Virginia landscape from Lance's helicopter and saw where his house should be, but the big trees cut off the view.

"A car will meet you at the Farm's pad and drive you to your house," Lance said.

"Farm?" Sally asked.

"It's the CIA training facility, Camp Peary," Ed replied, "though it won't look like that from above."

287

They set down on the pad, and their luggage was unloaded, including Ed's weapons. He wouldn't have been able to fly commercial with those, he reflected.

Lance shook hands with them both and waved them off in an armored SUV.

Shortly, as they reached the highway and turned right, Ed tapped the driver on the shoulder. "Keep it at a steady fifty and drive past the house," he said. "I want to get a good look at it before we commit."

The house appeared on their left and Ed could find nothing wrong. He was pleased that the grass had been mown by the teenager he employed for that purpose. "Okay," he said to the driver, "turn around at the convenience store ahead. This time we'll turn into the driveway, and you can be rid of us."

The man followed his instructions and stopped in the driveway. Ed asked Sally to wait, then got out of the car and, as he climbed the front steps, unholstered the handgun he was packing. He let himself quietly into the house and walked the whole place, looking for anything amiss. Finally, he went back to the car and fetched Sally, while the driver got the luggage inside and upstairs, then refused money and was gone.

"Ed, this is charming," Sally said, walking

around the rooms.

"Thank you, but stay away from the windows for the time being."

"I like you being cautious," she said.

"Life can be short when you're not cautious," he replied, then took her into the study and fixed her a drink, while he put away his weapons in the large safe, concealed in a room behind a bookcase. "There's space for us in here, should we need shelter," he said, showing her how to open and close the swinging bookcase.

"There's a car in the garage outside, should we need to run." He gave her his spare key.

"Where would I run?" she asked. "Anyway, you'd be with me."

"Assume I'm not, for the moment. Take the car in the garage, keys in kitchen drawer, turn right out of the driveway and get to the gate of the Farm, which will appear four and a half miles down the road. Turn in there, stop at the gate, identify yourself, and ask them to call Lance."

"Got it," she said.

"I ordered some groceries for dinner, and they should be delivered in an hour or so. I thought I'd grill some steaks."

"That sounds lovely."

"Let me check in with Stone." He sat

down next to her on the sofa and called.

"Yes?"

"It's Ed. We're at the intended place and still alive, but we're being careful. You should be, too."

"We were thinking of going out to dinner," Stone said.

"That's fine, if you want one of your favorite restaurants shot up and many of the other diners dead."

"Just when do you think we should start trusting the Greek and his people not to kill us?"

"Never," Ed said.

"We've got plenty of security on the ground, but you have none there, do you?"

"Not of the kind you mean," Ed said, "but I can fend them off until the cavalry arrives."

"What cavalry is that?"

"Lance and I have an arrangement that holds until we're both comfortable with the situation."

"How long do you think that will take?"

"Until the Greek starts to see how nice it is when nobody is trying to kill him. That feeling is the only thing between us and a firefight, or worse. If you want some free advice, I'd go back to Maine for a little while. It's off the Greek's turf, and you've got that fortified house to hole up in."

"That's not the worse advice I've ever had," Stone said.

"Good luck to us both." Ed hung up.

"Ed," Sally said.

"Yes, m'dear?"

"I hope you'll always be that blunt with me."

"Count on it," Ed replied.

45

It took Ed a long time to get to sleep that night, but the presence of the warm, svelte body in the bed next him eventually lulled him into a fitful doze. He woke whenever he heard the slightest noise, inside or outside the house.

He got out of bed at five AM as gingerly as possible, so as not to wake Sally. He hung his holster on the inside of the bathroom door, then shaved, showered, and dressed in his habitual civilian mode, khakis and a plaid shirt, fairly heavy boots with Vibram soles, and shoulder holster under a plaid vest, then he went downstairs and put sausages from the local butcher in a pan to fry. If that smell didn't wake Sally, nothing would.

Fifteen minutes later, as he was contemplating starting the eggs, she came into the room, looking bright and rested, her hair pulled back into a ponytail.

He kissed her hello. "How do you like your eggs?"

"Scrambled," she replied.

He knew what she meant: the British way. He scrambled and seasoned the eggs, then put them into a pan at a very low temperature, constantly stirring them with a spatula. He sprinkled over that a layer of grated Parmesan cheese and continued to stir, while he put English muffins into the toaster.

When the eggs were just past being runny, he put them onto warmed plates, where they continued to cook a bit from their own temperature, as he buttered the muffins. Finally, he added the sausages, poured two glasses of freshly squeezed orange juice, turned on the coffeepot, and set everything on the table. They breakfasted in near silence, which Ed took as a compliment on his cooking.

"You're not comfortable here," Sally said, finally. "Do you want me to go back to London?"

"You're right about your assertion and wrong about your question," he said. "Something inside me is keeping me from relaxing — like a faint alarm bell ringing."

"Then let's get out of here," she said.

"Right. Have you ever been to Maine?"

"No, never."

"Here's your chance. Get your gear together while I make a call or two."

A taxi drove them to a country airport not far from Ed's house, and a moment later, a Citation M2 light jet set down and taxied over to them. The single pilot loaded the luggage, while Ed answered a call.

"It's Stone."

"Are you still alive?" Ed asked.

"Alive and well."

"Not bound head and foot in a dank cellar somewhere?"

"Nope, but I've been thinking about your advice, and I'm going to take it."

"Good. We're about to take off, so I'll speak to you this evening." They hung up.

Two and a half hours later the M2 set down on the short runway on Islesboro, and Ed paid the pilot in cash and called the local taxi, while the aircraft taxied out and took off. It would stop for refueling at Rockland, then continue back to Virginia.

They stopped at the village store to pick up the groceries he had ordered. Then, as they approached Ed's house, he told the driver to stop, while he got out his iPhone and checked the cameras around the property, inside and outside the house. Then he told the driver to continue and used the phone to open his gate. "Turn around, point the car at the gate, and keep the engine running," Ed said, then he did a close inspection of the property and house. Satisfied that they were alone, he paid the driver and moved their luggage and groceries inside.

"Ed," Sally said, "this is not false praise, but I like this place even better than the one we just left."

"Then I'm happy," Ed said. "Unpack while I secure the place." He turned on the TV sets in the kitchen, bedroom, and living room and displayed the twelve outdoor cameras on each, then he opened his concealed gun closet and chose weapons to scatter about the house and property, so that he would never be far from one, should he need it.

While Ed did his work, Sally put away the groceries and made lunch. When they had finished, he called Stone.

"Hey."

"Where are you?"

"Just landed at Rockland, we're transferring to the Cessna, and we'll be home in less than an hour."

"We're safe and here. Call me to let me know that you made it, or I'll be over there, guns ablaze."

"Will do. Come to dinner, drinks at six?"

"Love to." Ed hung up. "We have a dinner invitation," he said to Sally. "It will most likely be lobster, so I hope you like that."

"I do."

"The TVs and my library are at your disposal," Ed said. "If you're watching TV and the picture suddenly turns to security cameras, that means somebody is nearby. If I'm napping, wake me."

"Yes, sir," she said, giving him a smart salute.

Ed settled into his reclining chair and was soon snoring softly. A half hour later he got a call from Stone saying they had arrived safely, then he went back to sleep.

Stone and Rocky settled into the master suite, while Dino and Viv made themselves comfortable down the hall; they would stay until Dino's office forced him to return.

Stone stretched out for a nap, when his cell phone rang, Joan calling. "Yes?"

"Are you there and safe?"

"Yes, thanks, we're fine."

"I've got a call for you on the other line. I thought you might want to talk to him."

"Whoozat?"

"Egon Pentkovsky."

296

"Where did you tell him I am?"

"Out of the country, no more."

"Put him through." There was a *click*.

"Mr. Barrington?"

"Yes, Mr. Pentkovsky, to what do I owe the pleasure?"

"I understand you're out of the country?"

"Yes."

"Where, may I ask?"

"On the move."

"Forgive me, if I intrude. Can you tell me when you'll be back?"

"I haven't decided."

"I have some rather urgent business I'd like to discuss with you — quite legitimate business."

"Mr. Pentkovsky, I think that, given my past interactions with your family, it would be inappropriate for me to represent you, your relatives, or your businesses."

"I'm sorry to hear that."

"Life is full of disappointments."

"My associate will be *very* disappointed."

"Please express my condolences and tell him to get over it."

Egon chuckled. "I'm afraid my associate will not share your sense of humor. In fact, he doesn't really have a sense of humor — not in English, anyway. The business I wish to discuss would be conducted directly with me and not with Serge. I have a sense of humor."

"I'm happy for you, Mr. Pentkovsky, but my previous statement fully expresses my reluctance to involve myself with any of your family, even your own charming self."

Pentkovsky laughed again. "You see?"

"Please excuse me, Mr. Pentkovsky, but you're standing between me and a glass of bourbon whiskey. I wish you a good day and a happy life." Stone hung up.

"Was that the Greek?" Rocky asked.

"That was Pentkovsky, the youngest."

"And he wanted you to represent him?"

"I think not. I think what he wants is my presence next to him, in a place where a sniper couldn't miss."

46

Ed drove past the Barrington house, then down the driveway to the local yacht club, along the shore, and back to the road. Not until then did he turn into Stone's driveway. As he did, a garage door opened, and Ed drove into it and secured the car, as the door slid shut behind him.

"I take it we're here," Sally said.

"We are. Before we go, let me tell you about this house."

"I take it I won't read about it in *Country Life* or *Town & Country.*"

"You will not. Stone had a cousin named Richard Stone — Dick."

"I believe I knew him. He was the CIA station chief in London, was he not?"

"You are correct. He was in line for director of operations, one notch away from director, when he built this house on Stone family land. Because of his importance to the Agency, the house was given what they liked to call 'the D treatment,' which is sort of a building code for secure structures. That means that the house, instead of being sheathed in plywood, before the shingles went on, was instead encased in half-inch steel plate; the roof, too. The windows are all triple-plate armored glass and the doors all of steel, lined with Kevlar fabric. The result is a building that could be penetrated only by the sort of ammo used in anti-tank weapons, which is not generally available in this state. Dick passed away — not on Agency business, a family affair — and Stone inherited the house."

"It sounds very cozy," Sally replied. "And reassuring."

"I'm glad you feel that way. Let's go inside."

They entered the house through a door to the entry gallery, where they were greeted by everyone.

"You folks appear to be a drink ahead of us," Ed said. "We'd like to catch up, if we may."

Stone did the honors and handed Ed his usual single malt Scotch and Sally one of his matchless vodka gimlets. "I've had contact with Pentkovsky," Stone said.

Ed gulped his first sip. "What sort of contact?"

"Relax, it was telephonic; Joan transferred the call and told him I was out of the country."

"Good move. What the fuck did he want?"

Stone related the conversation, as fully as he remembered it.

"I hope you didn't bite."

"I chewed and spat," Stone replied.

"How did young Egon take the news?"

"Pretty well, I think. Unlike Gromyko, he has a sense of humor, or so he told me."

"Somehow, I don't think you and I would find him funny."

"Probably not, but he does have charm."

"I wonder how many men young Egon has killed," Ed said.

"I don't know. What's your best guess?"

"A dozen or two," Rawls replied. "After all, he's young."

"You think we can expect a visit from them here?"

"I wouldn't be surprised," Ed said. "But me, rather than you. I'm ready for that. I don't know if they even know about your place."

"Well, if they do, they'll give us a little time to start feeling comfortable and letting our guard down."

"But we won't do that, will we?" Ed asked.

"Nope, we won't."

"I've told Sally about the construction qualities of your house."

"I was very impressed," Sally said. "I feel very comfortable here."

"And welcome, too," Stone said.

"Of course."

They all sat down before the fire and made their drinks go away, then Stone replaced them with fresh ones.

"You know," Ed said, "it doesn't seem the same without Lance."

They all laughed.

"That may have been funny," Ed said, "but it wasn't intended that way. Where Lance goes is quickly followed by very good security."

"Don't worry," Viv said. "A few of our people are out there somewhere."

Rocky spoke up. "Stone, did you hear helicopter rotors?"

"I did not. I think you're thinking too much about Lance."

The phone rang in the kitchen; someone answered it, said a few words, then hung up. Mary Hotchkiss, wife of Seth, the caretaker, came out of the dining room and put some more plates on the table.

"Uh-oh," Stone said.

"It couldn't be," Rocky replied.

302

Another few minutes passed before the doorbell rang. Stone stood up, and Ed with him. "Just a minute," he said.

"What?"

"That may not be Lance at the door."

People started moving about, producing weapons, and taking up defensive positions.

Stone whipped out his iPhone and pressed the security camera icon. "It's Lance," he said, putting the phone away. "Resume your former positions, while I let him in." He walked to the door, checked the peephole, and opened the door.

"Good evening, Stone," Lance said.

"Why, Lance, you are very nearly late for dinner. Please come in."

"No need to tell Mary I'm here," Lance said. "She knows."

Stone went to the bar and poured him a Scotch. "Have you come all this way, at government expense, just to satisfy your yen for Maine lobster?"

"Well, it is the best in the world, followed closely by that of Ireland."

"I don't believe I've ever had lobster in Ireland," Stone said, handing him his drink.

"That's because the French buy it all up before it can reach the restaurants," Lance replied. "On their menus they say it's from Brittany or Normandy."

"Deceitful of them," Stone commented. They sat down. "All right," he said to Lance, "tell us why you've come."

"Let me put it this way," Lance said. "I didn't come alone."

47

Stone heard the sound of another helicopter in the distance. "Don't worry," Lance said, "it's ours."

"And why did you think it was necessary?" Stone asked.

"Somebody out there, on his belly in the grass, spotted a truck coming from the direction of Searsport."

"Surely they wouldn't try that again," Stone said. "Not after the last result."

"They would," Lance replied, "only this time the name on the side is different, and it's an electrician's truck, from a company with no listing in the local phone book."

"We have a perfectly good electrician living on the island," Stone said.

"Of course you do."

"I take it you're going to tell us when we should scramble."

"Certainly," Lance replied, glancing at his watch. "The next ferry doesn't arrive for another fifty minutes."

"Dinner is served," Mary called from the kitchen door.

"I guess we have time for dinner, before the electrician's van arrives," Stone said.

"My people are here to be sure that it doesn't arrive," Lance said, "and I don't think we'll hear from them until we're drinking port. They'll need time to conduct an interrogation."

"I'd rather not think about that while dining," Stone said, rising. "Shall we heed the call?"

They had finished the port and Stilton and were gathered around the fire, on brandy, before Lance's phone rang. He stepped into the entry hall to take it, then came back, looking puzzled.

"What is it?" Stone asked.

"The interrogation has been completed," he said.

"With what result?"

"With the result that the two men inside — father and son, as it turns out — are electricians, and from Rockland, not Searsport. Their family has taken a rental house on the island for the season, and they were on their way home from a job in Lincolnville. All this has been corroborated."

"Well, Lance," Stone said, "I don't know how you're going to explain this to your bean counters back at Langley."

"Neither do I," Lance said. "Would it be inconvenient for me to have a bed for the night?"

"Not in the least. You may have the guest house — both of them if you'd like to sleep surrounded by an armed guard."

"I would prefer that," Lance said, checking his watch. "I should go to bed now, so as to be fresh for the morning flight home."

"Good night, then," Stone said.

"Please don't get up," Lance said to all. "Sleep well." He left through the kitchen.

"Well," Ed said, "that was disappointing. I thought there would be fireworks."

"I'm not disappointed," Dino said. "And I like the idea of sleeping while surrounded by heavily armed guards."

Shortly after Lance's retiring, Ed felt the need for his bed. Stone walked him out of the living room. "How do you want to handle this?" he asked.

Ed told him, then got Sally into the Jeep. "Please put your head in my lap, m'dear."

"Why, Ed, can't you wait until we're in bed?" she asked.

"Purely for protecting you," Ed said.

"Please don't lift your head, especially to look outside the Jeep, until I tell you we're clear."

"As you wish," she said, rearranging herself so that she could rest her head in his lap.

The garage lights went off, and the door slid softly up. Ed started the engine and flipped a switch he had installed that turned off the dashboard and brake lights. He reversed quickly out of the garage, then turned down the road toward home and shot forward. Then there was a crash.

"What was that?" Sally asked, gripping his thigh tightly.

"That was me turning too soon in the dark and taking out Stone's mailbox," Ed replied, accelerating. "I may have attracted attention. Do you mind keeping your head down until we're home?"

"I'm getting used to it," she replied. "I may doze off, if you don't hit any more mailboxes."

"You do that." Ed pulled over to the side of the road, under some large trees and switched on his iPad. "The coast is clear, as one adulterer said to another on the phone." He turned into his driveway, and the log gate was fully open by the time he got here. The motion-sensitive floodlights around the house and the dock came on for ten seconds, then went out. Ed used his remote to open the garage door and drove inside. Only when the door had firmly closed did he switch on the lights.

"Are we there yet?" Sally asked.

"We are there, but I'm enjoying your head in my lap."

"To be continued," she said, and they got out of the Jeep and went inside.

At Stone's house they all went upstairs to their rooms, and Stone took a checklist from a bedside drawer and went through it, turning off various lights with his iPhone. Finally, they were left with only the bedside lamps burning.

"What was that crash I heard outside right after Ed and Sally left?" Rocky asked.

"I think it was the sound of Ed's Jeep taking out my mailbox," Stone replied.

Rocky laughed. "Is he that bad a driver?"

"There are no exterior lights on the island, except on peoples' front porches, and those are mostly out by this time of night. Ed was driving without his headlights, and I don't think there's much of a moon; too cloudy."

"I'm glad he didn't meet someone going the other way, also without headlights."

"So am I," Stone said. "That would have

been a much noisier crash."

They stripped and got into bed.

"I'm impressed with how cool you all are, under the circumstances," Rocky said.

"Worrying is a waste of energy," Stone said. "I'd rather save it for you."

From somewhere in the distance came what sounded like a single shot from a hunting rifle.

"What was that?" Rocky asked.

"It sounded like a rifle shot," Stone replied.

"I hope it was Ed's," she said.

"So do I."

Stone's phone rang, and he picked it up from the bedside table. "Yes?"

"It's Ed; I just wanted you to know that the shot you heard was mine."

"What were you shooting at?"

"There was a slow-moving boat a quarter of a mile off my dock," Ed said. "I just put a round across her bows. She ran for it."

"I hope it wasn't the Coast Guard," Stone replied, then hung up.

48

Stone woke with sunlight streaming into the room and an empty bed beside him. He used the bathroom, then checked Rocky's, but she was not to be found. He slipped into a silk robe, walked downstairs, and called for her. No answer. Then he felt a bit of a breeze, which he thought was from the air-conditioning, until he looked toward the back porch and saw the rear door standing half open. His heart stopped.

He had two choices, he thought. He could run back upstairs and get his pistol, or he could open Dick's office and find something there. He retrieved the clump of keys from a sofa-side table drawer, let himself into the office, and chose the officer's Colt .45, checked the magazine and racked the slide, put on the safety, then went to the rear door. There was an assault rifle tucked behind the door, but he didn't want to go outside in broad daylight carrying it. He

311

could hear splashes and shrieks from some kids diving off the adjacent yacht club dock, and he stepped out onto the back porch, feeling exposed, his right hand in the robe's pocket on the pistol. He checked out the backyard and his dock, the Picnic Boat at its mooring. Nothing amiss. He was about to walk around the house when he heard a voice.

"Stone!"

He looked back toward the water and saw a hand waving at him just ahead of the boat's prow. There was a head attached to it. "Come here," she called.

Stone let his eyes play around the dock for other heads and saw none. He began to walk slowly toward the dock.

"Hurry up!" she called out, trying not to yell.

"Okay, I've got you," he called back and continued, not hurrying.

"It's very cold in here," she called. "Will you get a move on?"

"I don't want to attract attention," he said, as he got closer.

"Neither do I. I'm naked!"

He reached the dock. "I'll pull you out."

"No! Find me a towel."

"I'll check on the boat." He walked down the dock and jumped into the big cockpit

312

and had a look around, then returned. "Nothing there. Don't you have a bathing suit around here?"

"I didn't bring one," she said, "and I don't want to shock all those little boys and their mothers."

"All right, here's what we'll do," Stone said. "I'll stand with my back to the club dock and pull you out. Then, keeping between you and the dock, we'll walk unhurriedly up to the house."

"All right, but hurry up! I'm freezing."

Stone crossed his arms and reached down for her, then to her hands and, as he pulled her onto the dock, rotated her until her back was to him.

"Give me your robe," she said, shivering.

"I can't. I'm naked, too." He opened the robe and pulled her to him, then closed the robe around her. "Jesus! You're a living iceberg."

"Don't move," she said, backing all the way up to him. "It's going to take me a few minutes before I can walk."

"The hell it is," he said grabbing her shoulders and walking her up the catwalk to the backyard. In half a minute they were inside the back door. He kicked it shut, grabbed a cashmere throw from a chair, and wrapped it around her.

313

"Mary has laid a fire. I'll start it."

"Hurry!"

Stone went to the mantel, found a box of long matches, then reached down, turned on the gas jet, and tossed a lit match into the fireplace. It made a *whomp* noise and began to burn. Rocky elbowed him out of the way, opened the throw, and held her body as close to the fire as she could and turned herself like a chicken on a spit.

Stone sat down on the sofa and waited for her to thaw.

"Now," he said, "could you please tell me what you were doing in the bay, butt nekkid, in full sight of the yacht club dock?"

"Swimming," she said.

"You know, I was just elected to membership there, and I don't want to get thrown out the first week."

"I woke up and you were still sound asleep, so I had a look out the back, and it was deserted, so I ran down to the dock, dove in, and swam a ways out. It was cold but bearable, as long as I was swimming. Then I heard a screen door slam and a lot of voices, and when I looked around there were boys pouring out of the club."

"I think there's a sailing class, or something," he said.

"I made it back to the dock right before

you came out, and the boat had too much freeboard for me to climb aboard. I wanted to scream for you, but that would have attracted way too much attention. Then you came outside, and after a very long time, rescued me."

"I didn't want to run. That would have attracted attention, too."

She cast off the throw and sat down beside him. "There, now I'm warm and dry." She tugged at his robe. "And you're naked under there, aren't you?"

"I'll be naked when we get upstairs, too, and we won't have to worry about Mary coming into the room."

"I'll race you," she said, jumping up and running for the stairs.

Stone did the same.

Down the road apiece, Ed Rawls sat on his dock with his Czech sniper's rifle lying across his lap and looked out across Penobscot Bay. There was a small noise behind him, and he jerked around to find Sally there, wrapped in a blanket. "Young lady," he said, "don't go sneaking around like that. There could be disastrous consequences."

"Scoot over," she said, and he made room on the bench.

"Fishing?" she asked.

315

"Yeah, I want a big one, too."

"Have you seen the boat again?"

"There's something way out there," he said. "I saw a glimmer of something."

"Are you nervous, Ed?"

"Always. They're nervous, too. They're afraid to come in closer, and I like that."

"I'd rather they weren't there at all," she said.

"Me, too."

"If this were London, and I still had the job, I'd have a squad of coppers in combat gear scattered around."

"Well, this time, all you've got is me."

"I guess I'll just have to make do, then."

"I guess so."

"I'm glad I'm here and not in London," she said.

"Me, too. Do you think you could get used to it here?"

"Not year around," she said. "Brrrr!"

"I don't blame you."

"You know, Ed, I've got quite a bit of money from my late husband's estate. We could buy a place in Florida for the winters."

"I'm not crazy about Florida," he said, then he was quiet for a moment. "I like New York, though."

"That's a thought."

316

"I've got some money lying around, too," he said.

"Oh, good."

49

Stone was having an afternoon nap on a living room sofa when a phone rang. He opened an eye. It didn't sound like his cell phone. It rang a couple more times, and he realized it was the landline. He picked up a phone on the sofa-side table. "Hello?"

"Stone?"

A familiar voice, but he couldn't place it. "Yes?"

"It's Egon Pentkovsky — well, for a little longer, anyway."

"Oh?" Stone was fully awake now.

"I hope you're back in the country. I'm going to be in your neighborhood, house hunting, and I wondered if we could meet briefly."

"Haven't we already had this conversation?" Stone asked.

"*A* conversation. Not *this* conversation."

"How do the two differ?"

"My associate and I have had a parting of

the ways."

"Well, you must be the better shot, since you're talking to me."

"I don't shoot at people. I never have."

"Plenty of others to handle that for you, huh?"

"Never with my agreement. I'm very different from the rest of my family."

"In that case, let me ask you a question."

"Anything."

"Is Gromyko still alive?"

"Probably not."

"Why is there doubt in your mind about that? Don't you know how to find a pulse?"

"We are not in the same place," Egon said. "I mean, more than geographically."

"Where are you, geographically?"

"In Camden," Egon said. "Looking at houses."

"As an investment?"

"To live in. For the summers, anyway."

"And where is the Greek?"

"Very likely at the bottom of Sheepshead Bay," Egon said. "Not that I wish him ill."

"You two have parted company?"

"Very well put. We won't be seeing each other again."

"I'm confused."

"I know, it must be confusing. Look, I'm coming over to your island tomorrow morn-

319

ing, to look at a house there."

"Who's your real estate agent?"

"A fellow named Jimmy Hotchkiss. I understand he knows the island very well."

"That's an understatement," Stone said. "What house are you seeing?"

"It was previously occupied by a Caleb Stone, now deceased. Did you know him?"

"He was my first cousin."

"Then you know the house?"

"I spent a summer there when I was eighteen."

"What sort of place is it?"

"I think if you ask Jimmy that, he'd say it has good bones."

"That's exactly what he did say. He also said that it has undergone a major renovation."

"I didn't know that, but then, the house isn't visible from the road. Who renovated it?"

"An owner who bought it from the Stone estate, who himself died before it could be completed. Now his estate is selling."

"What are they asking?"

"Three million."

"If it's a good renovation, it would be worth that, I think. You might get it for less." Why am I having a perfectly normal conversation about real estate with this guy? he asked himself.

"I wonder if I could drop by your place around two PM? Jimmy will know where it is, yes?"

"Jimmy knows everything about everybody. If you're going to buy here, you'd better get used to that."

"May I see you then?"

"Who else is coming?"

"I'll be alone. My wife and two girls will be joining me in a couple of days."

"What are we going to talk about?"

"I hope I can ask your advice about some things."

Stone was overcome with curiosity. "All right, two o'clock tomorrow."

"Thank you. I'll see you then. Oh, by the way, I'm changing my surname to Greco, my mother's maiden name, and I've already started using it. That's how Jimmy will know me."

Smart move, Stone thought, if he's on the level. "See you then, Mr. Greco." They hung up.

Stone got himself a glass of lemonade from the kitchen, to get his blood sugar up again, then he went to Dick's office and called Lance on that line.

"Is everything all right, Stone?" Lance asked.

"I think so, but I've just had a weird phone call from Egon Pentkovsky, who is calling himself 'Greco' these days. I'd like to know everything I can about him before two PM tomorrow, which is when he is coming to meet me." He told Lance the details of their conversation.

"I'm not sure that 'weird' is sufficient to describe that conversation," Lance said. "Let me see what I can find out."

"Okay, and see if you can find a recent live sighting of the Greek, will you? I'd especially like to know if he's dead. Egon says he may be."

"Oh, yes." Lance hung up.

There was a rap on the door and Rocky stuck her head in. "You disappeared on me."

"I'm sorry, I woke up, then couldn't get back to sleep, so I came down here." He brought her up to date on his conversation with Egon. They went back to the living room and took a sofa.

"Do you think Egon might be bringing reinforcements?"

"He's bringing Jimmy Hotchkiss. He said his wife and two daughters will be here in a couple of days."

"And this is the house where the evil twins once lived?"

"Yes, my cousin Caleb's twin boys are

housed at the Maine State Prison, serving, I think, a dozen or so consecutive life sentences for murder. If they ever get out, Connecticut and Massachusetts would also like to speak to them."

"I want to hear that story. Where is the state prison?"

"In Warren, not very far from here."

"Then tell me the story when we're out of the state. I don't want those boys in my head."

"Good move," Stone said. "I won't enjoy telling you the story, since they are my only living cousins."

Dino came into the room in time to hear the last snatch of that conversation. "You're right, Rocky. You don't want to hear that story while you're here."

"Now I'm getting curious," Rocky said. "You two don't often agree, but you agree on that."

"We do," Stone said.

"It's not the sort of story you can disagree on. You know, a book has been written about those boys, and I saw a copy around here somewhere. It's called *Dark Harbor*."

"I saw it, too," she said. "I'll find it and read it on the way home."

"That will save me a lot of painful recounting."

50

Lance didn't call back until the following morning, after breakfast. "Sorry about not getting back to you sooner, but I got sidetracked."

"What have you learned about Egon Pentkovsky Greco?" Stone asked.

"Not a hell of a lot," Lance replied. "That's why I didn't call sooner. I kept thinking there should be more, but there wasn't."

"Gimme whacha got!" Stone said.

"All right: born thirty-four years ago in Greenwich, Connecticut, local schools, followed by Groton, Yale, with a bachelor's in accounting and business management, and Yale Law School, JD. Never practiced law, as such, but the degree helped him in advancement at Webb & Westfield, a largish New York accounting firm, now defunct. Mr. Westfield's work habits consisted mostly of bringing in new business, then stealing from the clients. He is still in prison, in his seventh year of a twenty-year sentence."

"Was Egon involved in any of that?"

"An investigation by the state authorities failed to provide any evidence to that effect. He mostly dealt with clients in the small-business sector of the firm's client roster, and Westfield stole only from the bigger ones. He bailed out of the firm a year before it crashed and opened an office of his own, representing a couple of dozen businesses that, by our estimation, were operated by his three brothers, two of them no longer extant, as you know. He closed his office less than a week ago, and he has a net worth of ten million dollars, or so. His wife is from an extremely wealthy family, and her trusts matured when she was twenty-five, some six years ago, so the couple is very well-fixed. They live in a large townhouse in the East Sixties. They have two daughters, seven and nine, who attend a fancy school for girls in New York. He owns and flies a Citation CJ3-Plus, as you once did, I believe. A Mr. E. Greco is currently registered at an inn in Camden."

"It that it? No murders, rapes, or parking tickets?"

"None. He's as clean as a bird's beak — on paper, at least. He appears, with the closure of his office, to have severed all ties with his associate, except through the businesses that are his clients."

"I confess I'm baffled as to why he wants to meet with me."

"I, as well. I suppose the thing to do is to take him at face value, a wealthy gentleman seeking the advice of another on the purchase of an island property."

"Then that's how I will receive him," Stone replied, and they ended their conversation.

Stone had finished lunch and was reading a novel, and Rocky was taking a nap upstairs, when the doorbell rang. Stone checked his watch: two o'clock, straight up. He found Egon Greco, né Pentkovsky, standing alone at the door and let him in.

"Jimmy Hotchkiss dropped me off. He'll come back for me after he runs an errand." He handed Stone a *New York Times*. "He asked me to give you this, to save you a trip to the store."

Stone admitted him and Mary brought them each a glass of her lemonade.

"I've seen the Caleb Stone house," Egon said. "I would say that the renovation, now a day or so from completion, is a high-quality one."

"Then it should make a very nice family home. Do you know if it was insulated? It never was before."

"Yes, and new heating and air-conditioning installed. Lovely kitchen, built by an island cabinet shop."

"I know their work," Stone replied. "It's good."

"Stone, can you think of any reason why I shouldn't make an offer on the property today?"

"None," Stone replied.

"I'm concerned, this being a small community, that any word of your difficulties with my family not become common knowledge."

"Not from me," Stone said. "And you're changed your name."

"That was easy. Greco was my middle name, after my mother."

"Do your girls go to school with any children who summer on the island?"

"They do not, as best as I can tell."

"Do you have any more questions of me about local real estate or life on the island?"

"No, Jimmy has not stopped talking about all that since I arrived."

Stone laughed, then got serious. "Now we come to the real reason for your visit," he said.

Egon nodded. "Let's call it an additional subject."

"I'm all ears."

"I want you to know that my associate may not keep his end of the truce that you proposed and he accepted."

"Oh?"

"In my business, grudges die hard. In fact, now that I think of it, I've never known a grudge to die at all."

"Perhaps you can tell me what this grudge is about," Stone said. "I've never been able to figure it out."

"It goes back to Paris some years ago, when you became entangled with some members of the Russian organization, resulting in the demise of some of its members."

"I remember it well. I thought it ended with their deaths."

"Not while my associate is alive."

"Is he still alive? On the phone you were doubtful of that."

"I still am. In fact, if he is not still alive, I am the instigator of his death."

"That sounds like the beginning of a grudge to me."

"My resigning from business with Gromyko was grounds for the grudge. I have made it known to someone who handles these things that I would like him to disappear from my life."

"And his, as well?"

"As well."

"Have you taken any steps to protect yourself and your family?"

"Moving here for the remainder of the summer is one step. If Serge survives until the late autumn I will have to rethink."

"Then, I take it, the person you spoke to is on the island?"

"He is."

"Would he be your cabinetmaker?"

Egon's eyes widened. "How would you know that?"

"I was a policeman in a former existence," Stone said, "and I met him while investigating some murders on the island. Oh, he was not the murderer, but I did come to know that he had done that sort of work in his youth, before moving up here to take over his late father's business."

"I see."

"Do you intend for him to do his work on the island?"

"Yes, but only if the Greek appears here."

"Are you expecting him?"

"Yes, but that's only my guess. You should let your friend Rawls know that he may be on his way."

"Why would he come himself, rather than sending someone?" Stone asked.

"Because it's personal with him, where both you and I are concerned. He would take pleasure in our deaths, and that of Rawls."

A horn tooted from outside.

"That would be Jimmy," Egon said.

Stone walked him to the door. "Thank you for the warning," Stone said.

"Good luck," Egon replied.

"You, too," Stone said, and watched him walk to Jimmy's car.

51

Stone had hardly sat down with his book again when there was a knock at the front door, followed by the doorbell. It sounded urgent; he got up and answered it.

Ed Rawls brushed past him. "What the hell is going on?" he demanded.

"Take it easy, Ed."

"Easy? Wasn't that Egon Pentkovsky who just left here with Jimmy?"

"It was."

"Was anybody killed?"

"No. Egon continues to abide by our truce and has taken other steps to distance himself from Gromyko." Stone sat him down, gave him a Scotch, and told him about his conversation with Egon.

"You believe that?" Rawls asked, thunderstruck.

"I did, and much of it is backed up by Lance's research into Egon. He's changed his name from Pentkovsky to Greco, his mother's maiden name. And did I mention that he's buying a house here, perhaps as we speak?"

Rawls's expression had not changed. "What house?"

"Caleb Stone's family place."

"I thought that had already been bought by somebody."

"It was, but the buyer died, and Egon is buying it from his estate. It's been completely renovated, partly by our friend, the cabinetmaker, whose reputation has preceded him with Egon. Both his reputations, I should say. Egon has asked him to kill Gromyko, if he comes on the island."

"Horseshit!"

"I don't have any reason not to believe him," Stone said. Ed was quieting down now, what with the Scotch plying his veins.

"What are you thinking of doing, Ed?"

"Taking the first shot," Ed replied firmly.

"Egon's wife and children are arriving tomorrow."

"Oh, swell, he's going to hide behind his family."

"Ed, could I point out that Egon has never done anything to you? It was you, after all, who took out two of his brothers."

"I did that for my country," Ed said.

"If I may ask, how much did your country

pay you for your work?"

"That's irrelevant," Ed said. He may have blushed a little.

"Ed, if anybody takes a shot at you, or otherwise threatens your existence, then you would have every right to defend yourself."

"You're goddamned right I would."

"However, you don't have the right to sneak over to the man's new house and kill him."

Ed sat back on the sofa and drained his glass. "So I have to give him the first shot, huh?"

Stone refilled his glass. "He's not going to shoot you, Ed."

"Listen, there's been a boat cruising up and down off my dock."

"How far off your dock?"

"I don't know, three, four hundred yards, maybe."

"It's Penobscot Bay, Ed; the largest such body of water in Maine, and it's full of boats, many of them cruising or fishing off your dock a few hundred yards. Don't take it personally."

"Was I supposed to take the guys in the plumber's van personally?"

"I believe you did, and they are no longer a threat."

"The guy who sent them is."

"Well, I'm afraid Egon thinks that is true."

"He said Gromyko is coming after us?"

"Words to that effect, and it was just a guess on his part."

"Who better to guess?"

"You have a point, but believe me, Egon is out of it. I think you can get away with shooting anybody else who comes after you."

"Gee, thanks."

"But not Egon. Just think of his wife and those two little girls, staring at you from a courtroom bench. You wouldn't have a chance with a jury."

"I'd blow my brains out, rather than go to prison," Rawls said.

"Or, you could just do everybody a favor and do that now. It would save a lot of trouble."

Rawls looked at Stone sharply. "You're a real pal, you know that?"

"I'm just trying to help, to keep you from murdering an innocent man who is going to be your neighbor."

"I don't know if I can sleep, knowing that he's just down the road."

"Give it a shot — and I mean that metaphorically. Is Sally going to stay for a while?"

"She is," Rawls said, and managed a little smile.

"She's a great reason to stay out of prison, Ed."

"And a great reason to stay alive," he said.

"Go home and take a nap, and make love to Sally. She will prefer that to conjugal visits at the Maine State Prison, and it will improve your mood."

"That's the best advice you've ever given me," Rawls said, then tossed off his drink and left.

52

Stone went upstairs to wake Rocky for dinner, and she wasn't in bed. He checked the bathroom, then went back downstairs and found her sitting on the sofa before the fire.

"You have quite a disappearing act," Stone said.

"While you were talking with your guests I took a nap, then I went out for a walk, and when I came back you were gone," she said.

"Now you're back."

"I am, and ready for a drink. It's sundown somewhere."

Stone made them both one. "There's something I have to tell you about," he said.

"Shoot."

"We're not out of the woods yet with the Greek." He told her about his conversation with Egon.

"Does he have any concrete knowledge of that?"

"Just what he reads into his conversations with Gromyko. It's his feeling that the Greek is going to disregard the pact he made with us and resume his worst intentions."

"I see."

"My point is, you should not go for walks alone."

"You don't think I can take care of myself?"

"Let me tell you a little story. Some years ago, the summer I inherited this house, a female friend of mine — one who shall remain nameless, but who is just as smart and capable of self-defense as you — went for a run down the road out there, where she was attacked without warning and spent four days bound, gagged, and chained to an iron bedstead, living on a diet of candy bars. She was about to be executed when we found her."

"Would she have a name familiar to me?"

"We won't discuss her name or her plight further. I use this story to show that when someone wants to get you, they can get you anywhere, even on this Edenic island. And it will save me endless worry if you will comply with my request."

"Even if I go armed?"

"She was armed."

"Ah."

"I'm waiting for an affirmative reply."

"What is the alternative?"

"To pack you up and put you on the nearest public conveyance, a Greyhound bus, and send you back to New York, where Lance will have you locked in the cellar of the Agency's New York station until this is resolved."

"You make it sound so attractive."

"It does have the advantage of giving you a long, long tour of the part of New England that is serviced by U.S. Highway Route One, which sports about three thousand traffic lights and stop signs on a two-lane road. The scenery is gorgeous, but take along three or four novels."

She sighed. "As difficult as that option is to resist, I will comply with your request."

"Oh, good. Let me top that drink up for you."

"Is this leading up to sex?" she asked, accepting the refill.

"Not until after dinner, unless you want to run the risk of being caught *in flagrante delicto* by other guests and passing strangers."

"I think I'll just keep drinking, until you're ready to throw me over your shoulder and haul me upstairs."

"Good choice."

The following morning Stone woke to find himself alone again, but before he could conduct a search, Rocky came out of the bathroom, dabbing at her hair with a towel, but otherwise naked, which he preferred.

"Have I ever told you you have a beautiful body?" he asked.

"And will I hold it against you?" she replied, supplying the punch line to an old joke.

"If you please."

"It's wet right now, but I'll get back to you on that." She went back into the bathroom and hair dryer noises began.

Mary rang a bell downstairs, inviting all to breakfast, so Stone got dressed and ran downstairs. Rocky followed shortly.

"Do I hear a helicopter?" Rocky asked.

Stone listened. "You do, I believe."

"Are we expecting VIPs?"

"I'm not," Stone replied. "But I think I hear two helicopters."

"Are we being invaded?"

"I hope not."

Seth came into the room. "You want me to drive to the airport?"

"Good idea," Stone said. "If the pas-

339

sengers are friendly, bring them back with you. If not, keep going." Seth disappeared.

Twenty minutes later, he walked back into the house. "Welcome back. No new house-guests arrived?" Stone asked.

Seth shook his head and described the helicopter he'd seen. "I didn't get a good look at the passengers, who had a taxi waiting for them, but the machine was a very slick corporate type."

"I don't much like the sound of that," Stone said, and he went to find Dino and fill him in.

53

Stone was still thinking about the helicopter when his phone rang.

"Yes?"

"It's Rawls. A chopper just flew by me at low altitude and landed."

"So Seth told me."

"I'm going to arm myself to the teeth and hunker down. I recommend you do the same."

"Right." Stone hung up.

"You think the Greek was aboard the chopper?" Dino asked.

"Helicopters are rare up here. No resident would land in one, since the town council has banned them from landing at the airfield: too noisy for local tastes."

"Then I think we should assume that we have company," Dino said.

"Then let's prepare a reception," Stone said. He unlocked Dick's little office and opened the weapons locker. "What would you like, Dino?"

"I'm carrying a Glock, so a long gun would make me happy."

"Me, too," Rocky said, "if I'm invited to the party."

"Come get ammo," Stone said to them. He issued the weapons, and they started loading magazines.

"You got any grenades in there?" Dino asked.

"Nope. I think Dick probably thought a grenade would be too contained in this house and destroy everyone's eardrums." He handed them the two assault rifles and chose the Heckler & Koch machine gun for himself, sticking magazines in his belt for ready access.

Thus armed to the teeth, they double-bolted all the doors and took up positions behind furniture.

"We've got armored glass in the windows, right?" Dino asked.

"Yes," Stone replied. "But I'd stay at the edges. We don't know what they're carrying."

Seth came into the room carrying a pump shotgun. "Mary is secure in the pantry," he said, "and I've got two boxes of double-ought shells." He set them on the coffee table and started stuffing his pockets with them.

There was a hammering on the front door, and Stone picked up a phone and pressed the intercom button. "Yes?"

"Police! We got a search warrant, open up!"

"What police?"

The man hesitated. "State cops!"

"I know the state cops around here. Identify yourself!"

More hesitation. "I am Brown!"

"I didn't ask what color you are. Who are you?"

"This is who I am," the voice yelled, and somebody started firing at the front door, which hardly noticed.

Stone turned and faced the rear picture window, figuring they would try that next.

A large man, fully suited up in black combat gear, ran onto the back porch, firing at the rear door.

Stone aimed at the door, in case it gave. It did not. The assailant stepped back out of sight.

"I don't think they knew what they'd be dealing with," Stone said to Dino, who was still covering the front door.

"Tough," Dino said.

Stone saw a black projectile come from

the side of the house and heard it bounce once on the rear porch. "Grenade!" he shouted. "Take whatever cover there . . ."

The explosion cut him off, but the door and big window held. Stone waited for the smoke to clear, then ran to the window, staying low, and looked from side to side. "Here he comes again!" he shouted, and hit the deck.

The assailant began firing at the rear door again and this time something penetrated the glass. "A round made it through!" he shouted. "Everybody, ready to fire at the door!"

What sounded like a sledgehammer struck the rear door, which held until the fourth or fifth attempt, then the doorframe seemed to bulge. "Watch out for another grenade!" Stone shouted. A moment later it went off. Astonishingly, the door held, and the man started to work with the sledgehammer again. What sounded like a crowbar was prying at the doorjamb. "He's going to get in in a minute," Stone cried. As he spoke, the door gave way and the man in black burst into the room.

All three of them fired bursts at him, and Stone's caught him low, under the knee, and the assailant fell forward onto his belly. Stone fired a burst at his ass, figuring the armor didn't go down that far at the rear. That got a cry and some swearing in a strange language from the man, and Stone fired another burst.

Dino ran forward, his Glock in his hand. He held the pistol at the back of the man's neck, under his helmet, and fired once. The man went limp.

"One down," Dino said.

Now the sledgehammer sounds came from the front door, and they spun around and concentrated on that. After a dozen tries the hammering stopped. Out of the corner of his eye, Stone saw another black-suited man headed for the rear door, firing as he ran. "Man at the back door!" he yelled, and everybody poured lead in that direction. The man's face mask blew away and blood spurted out.

"Two down!" Dino shouted, and everything went quiet.

"Stone," he heard Rocky say.

He turned and found her lying on her back, her chest bloody.

"Watch the back door!" Stone shouted and ran to Rocky's side. "Hey, girl, I'm here," Stone said to her. She blinked her eyes a few times and tried but failed to speak.

Stone had to calm himself and think for a

minute. Civilian 911 wasn't going to get here fast enough. He called the state police and asked for the guy he knew.

"Stone?"

"We're under heavy armed assault, and a woman here has taken a chest wound. We need a chopper at the Islesboro airfield stat!"

"We're on it!" the sergeant said.

"Bring fully suited men and the heaviest weapons you can manage. They've got automatic weapons and grenades."

"Departing now," the sergeant said, then hung up.

"Dino, you watch the back door. Seth, cover my back at the front door. I'm going to look for opposition. When we're clear, put the rear seats down for Rocky."

Mary came out of the kitchen with a stack of clean dishcloths and applied one to Rocky's chest, making encouraging noises. Stone flipped on the TV and used his iPhone to turn on all the cameras. Why hadn't he done that before? He did a quick survey of the front of the house, then went to Rocky and picked her up in his arms. "Seth, the station wagon!"

Seth opened the garage door, and Stone followed. They got the seats down, and Stone crawled into the back with Rocky.

"Hang on," he whispered in her ear. "We're on our way to the chopper."

Seth got the garage door open and the engine started.

Dino leapt into the shotgun seat, and they were on their way.

54

Ed Rawls sat inside his battened-down house; rolled-down steel shutters covered every window. Sally was loading magazines while Ed watched his twelve views of the property on TV. He could see no one. He called Stone's cell and got no reply. Oh, shit, he thought. "Stone, it's Ed; call me when you can. Let me know if you need anything." He hung up.

Ed looked at the image from the camera covering his dock and used the joystick on his iPhone controller to pan Penobscot Bay, then zoomed in on an approaching boat. It was a lobsterman's boat, but he didn't know who was driving it. He knew that some of the lobster boats could do 40 to 60 knots. They raced them in the bay. The boat grew larger on his screen.

Stone lay in the rear of the old Ford wagon, cradling Rocky in his arms, whispering encouragement in her ear. They were parked on the ramp near the runway, and he could hear a chopper approaching, but whose was it?

Dino stood at the edge of the runway. "We're okay, Stone. It's the state cops!"

"Hang on, Rocky, they're landing."

The chopper set down and four combat-suited men carrying assault rifles hopped onto the runway. Stone and Seth got Rocky out, while men on the chopper handed out a stretcher. They loaded the stretcher, but a large man barred Stone's way.

"No room for anybody but the wounded," he shouted over the noise of the spinning rotors.

Stone grabbed the rim of his flak jacket and pulled him close. "Listen to me!" he shouted. "She's going to die, and I don't want her to be alone! Leave two men. They're needed here!" The man nodded, pushed Stone into a canvas seat, buckled his seat belt, and handed him a headset. Stone adjusted it, then held Rocky's hand as they lifted off.

Ed spotted a rifle barrel protruding from the cockpit of the lobster boat, and the driver was wearing a helmet and combat mask. He went to his weapons locker and

349

pulled a rocket-propelled grenade launcher and fastened a round to it. He checked the monitor again, and saw the lobster boat was pulling into his empty dock, as he had hoped it would. His own boat was in the boathouse.

"Sally," he said, "I've got to go out onto the porch for a couple of minutes. You stop loading and get a weapon ready, should somebody breach a door. And for Christ's sake, don't shoot me; I'm the one in the red flannel shirt."

"Don't worry about me, Ed," Sally said, picking up an assault rifle and shoving a magazine into it.

Ed checked his monitors one last time, then raised a front window shade a couple of inches and looked out at the dock. They were ten meters out. He was only going to get one shot at this, he thought, as he opened the front door and stepped out onto the porch. He leaned against an upright and brought the weapon up to its firing position, sighting in on the boat, a little forward of the cockpit, in line with the driver. As they coasted in close to the dock, Ed judged their distance at forty yards. He was going to have to be accurate. He took a breath, let half of it out, and slowly squeezed the trigger.

350

■ ■ ■ ■

The state police helicopter settled onto the hospital pad, and Stone helped unload the stretcher. Two men grabbed the sheet under Rocky and lifted her onto their gurney, which had the advantage of wheels. They tried to brush Stone aside, but he held on to Rocky's hand and trotted alongside the gurney. They crashed through a set of double doors and picked up speed on the smooth, tiled floor. Stone could see two people down the hallway ahead of them, both fully garmented for surgical work, standing outside a door with an overhead sign reading TRAUMA 1. A doctor stopped them, got the bandage out of the way, and took a quick look at Rocky's chest. "OR 2, straight ahead! They're ready for her."

As they turned through the swinging doors of the operating room, a gowned nurse stepped between Stone and the gurney. "You can't help her anymore," she said to him. "Let us do our work." She pointed at a steel stairway. "You can see from up there."

Stone ran up the stairs and found himself on the upper level of a theater. He saw them lift Rocky onto the table, and two nurses began cutting off her clothes. There were now a half dozen gowned people clustered around Rocky, and they were connecting her to all sorts of equipment, which now came to life, and an anesthesiologist was injecting something into her IV tube. Stone centered his gaze on one screen, which seemed to be displaying her heartbeat.

To him, at least, it looked erratic.

Ed kept his eye glued to the telescopic sight and watched the rocket-propelled grenade fly. He wished he had time to load another round, but he couldn't stop watching. The grenade struck the side of the boat about eight inches below the gunwale, just aft of the driver's position, and the boat exploded. Ed could feel the hot air sweep over him, but he clung to the weapon. Suddenly, a voice from behind startled him. "Can you use this?"

Ed spun around to find Sally standing there, holding another round. He looked back at the boat. Pieces of it and of black-suited men were falling into the water and onto the dock. "Thank you," he said to Sally, "but I don't think I'll need it."

From out on the bay, a half dozen boats had turned toward his dock and were converging.

■ ■ ■

Stone watched from above as they draped Rocky's body, and a surgeon called for something. A scalpel larger than Stone had expected was slapped into his hand, and he stepped forward, his body shielding Rocky's from Stone's sight, for which he was grateful. He saw the man's elbow move as he made the cut into flesh Stone loved.

There was a plastic trash can near Stone's feet. He picked it up and vomited into it. This, he thought, is why they don't let civilians stay with the patient.

Then there came an extra-loud continuous beep from the equipment, and the display of Rocky's heartbeat flatlined. There was much movement and shouting among the attending medics. An assisting surgeon stepped forward with paddles and applied them to Rocky's chest. "Clear!" he yelled. Everyone took a step back, and Rocky's body arched, then collapsed back onto the table.

The display was still flatlining.

55

Stone gripped the railing of the tier where he watched, gritted his teeth, and muttered, "Come on, Rocky, come on!" As if in response to his pleading, the screen began to beep and display her heartbeats. Stone heaved a long sigh.

The surgeon was back at work, and Stone was relieved that he couldn't see what the man was doing. He watched for nearly an hour, then the surgeon stepped back and shucked off his gloves. "Close, Harry, will you?" He left the theater.

Stone ran down the stairs and found the entrance to the prep room. The young surgeon had shucked his cap and gown, too, and was bending over a sink, splashing water on his face. He saw Stone and turned to look at him. "What can I do for you?"

"I'm with her," Stone said, nodding toward the OR. "Tell me as much as you can."

"She took a single round to her chest,

where it missed her heart but nicked an artery. We were able to repair that and some other damage. The good news is, she's stable."

"How long before you'll know more?"

"She's in an induced coma, and she won't wake up until sometime tomorrow. Then she'll tell us how she is."

Stone looked at his watch.

"Right now," the doctor said, "I think she's in better shape than you are. She's not going to know you're here until at least twenty-four hours from now. Since there's nothing you can do here, I suggest you use the time to get some rest and food. Sleep if you can and come back at noon tomorrow. Maybe you'll be here when she wakes up."

"What if she doesn't wake up?"

"If she arrests, there'll be a team all over her to get her heart started again. You can't help with that. If you leave me a cell number, I'll call you if, and only if, there's any change. Don't call me. I need some rest myself."

Stone found a pad. "What's your name and number?"

"Paul Krause." He dictated a number.

"May I ask you a rude question, Dr. Krause?"

"As long as you don't expect a polite

355

answer."

"All right. If you were in her condition, who is the one doctor in the world within flying distance that you'd want attending you, because I can have him here in a few hours."

"There is such a physician," Krause said.

Stone got a pen ready. "What's his name?"

"Paul Krause. And she's lucky to have him."

Stone nodded. "I can accept that. Thank you, Doctor. By the way, the people who shot her are very likely to try again. Can you arrange security for her?"

"After a fashion, but hospital people are not armed. The state police are your best hope, unless you know of a topnotch security company nearby."

"Thank you, I do." Stone got on the phone to Mike Freeman and told him about Rocky's condition. "What can you do?"

"Hang on a minute." Stone could hear computer keys being tapped. "I've got four people in Portsmouth with a chopper. They can be there in less than an hour. I'll send four more from New York to the island, arriving in the morning."

"Great!"

"What about you, Stone?"

"I've got to check on the house and Ed

356

Rawls. When your people arrive at the hospital, can your chopper give me a lift to the island?"

"Of course. Keep the bird for as long as you like."

"Thanks, Mike." Stone went into the hallway and approached the nurse's station.

She saw him coming. "You can't see her now, sir, but she's in room 221, a floor up, for later reference."

"There will likely be people coming to hurt her, so don't give anyone else that room number. There will be four armed professionals here in less than an hour, and they'll identify themselves as being from a company called Strategic Services. Please tell them where to find her room." He wrote down his number. "If anybody else asks for her room number, give them a wrong number, then call the state police and me."

The sergeant and his chopper were waiting on the pad, when Stone got there.

"How is she?"

"Stable, and in an induced coma. More news tomorrow. Some Strategic Services people are choppering in later; can your guys guard her room until they come?"

"They are already doing so. Do you need a lift back to the island?"

"You're a mind reader. We also need as

many men as you can spare; we killed at least two of the intruders at my house, but we've no idea how many more there might be." The sergeant nodded, then made a winding motion with his finger, and the pilot jumped in and started engines.

"I'll send him straight back," Stone said, running for the copter. "Can you call Dino and tell him I'm on the way, and to meet me?"

"Sure, I've got his number."

Stone hopped into the aircraft and strapped in. The only other person he needed to call was Lance, but there was too much noise to use his phone. The chopper rose, climbed, and turned for Islesboro.

Twenty minutes later, the machine set down on the runway, and Dino and Viv were waiting with the station wagon. Stone thanked the pilot and ran for the car. Dino already had it running.

"How's Rocky?" Dino asked.

"Stable, and on the mend, I hope. Have you heard anything from Ed Rawls?"

"Not a word."

Stone called Ed's house.

"Be quick about it," Ed said.

"It's Stone. What's your condition?"

"Safe. I can't say the same for a boat that

tried to dock here, loaded with ninjas."

"Did any of them get ashore?"

"Not in one piece. There are body parts here and there."

"Jesus, Ed, what did you use on them?"

"RPG. Worked good."

"Rocky took a round and has survived surgery. I'm back on the island. You got any ideas?"

"I've got an idea the Greek is somewhere nearby, but we haven't heard from him yet. You want to come here? We're snug and well-armed."

"Yes. We're not far away, in the Ford station wagon. We need to check on Seth and Mary first, though."

"I'll crack my shell when I see you on camera. Drive right in through both gates, then I'll button up again."

Stone hung up. "Have you got any idea where my machine gun is?"

"On the back seat. I hope you've got ammo."

"Let's look in on Seth and his wife, then we'll go to Ed's place; he's got everything, including a grenade launcher, minus one round. He used that to take out an invading boat. Nobody survived." Dino turned into Stone's drive.

He found Seth and Mary in the living

room, working on the back door. "Are you two okay?"

"We will be, when I get this door up, and if they don't have more grenades."

"I'll be at Ed Rawls's house. Call if you need me." He got back into the car. "They're fine," he said to Dino, who got the car in gear and headed down the road.

"Here comes Ed's driveway. Drive in slowly, so he can ID us."

Dino turned into the driveway, and the fallen-log gate started to move, then they were through the second gate. "Look at that," Dino said, pointing at the smoldering ruin of a vessel moored there.

"I can see why nobody survived."

They got out of the car, and were greeted by Sally, on the porch, bearing an AK-47.

56

The inside of Rawls's place looked like a charming Maine house, with an armory overlaid. There were a dozen loaded weapons lying around and magazines of different calibers stacked neatly on the dining room table. Stone helped himself to some for his machine gun.

"Some lunch?" Sally asked.

"I'd love that," Stone said, "but first I have to call Lance." He did so.

He answered immediately. "I understand that Rocky is injured but stable," Lance said.

"I understand that, too. Have you ever heard of a surgeon called Paul Krause?"

"Certainly, the best thoracic surgeon in the United States, possibly in the world."

"I'm relieved to hear it."

"You're at Rawls's place?"

"I am."

"I hear that Gromyko is on the island with as many as a dozen men."

361

"Swell. We've knocked out about half of them."

"Splendid; keep going."

"Is Egon Pentkovsky part of this?"

"Greco. He's in Camden, awaiting his family. They have a real estate closing tomorrow, I believe."

"So I don't have to look out for him?"

"I shouldn't think so. What do you need from me?"

"Nothing that you could get here right now," Stone said. "I've already asked the state police for all the people they can spare."

"They have a ferry reservation for a truck in an hour or so," Lance said. "That might be who you're looking for."

"Good. I could use some aerial surveillance of the island, too, particularly around Rawls's house."

"I'll see if I can redirect a satellite," Lance said. "It could take a couple of hours, though. My chopper is at the hospital, looking for you; he might be of help."

"Sorry, I got another ride."

"I'll ask him to supply you with as much surveillance as he can. What's the radio frequency of the Islesboro airfield?"

"It's 122.9."

"Cells don't always work, but the radio

362

should. I expect Ed has one; he has every-thing."

"I wish I were as well-informed as you, Lance."

"You are, now."

They both hung up.

Sally handed him a bowl of beef stew, and he dug in.

"I always keep a stew on hand, just in case," she said. "And *just in case* seems to happen all the time around here."

A buzzer went off, and one of the screens started flashing. Ed stopped the noise and peered at the screen.

"I don't see anything," Stone said.

"Likely a deer," Rawls replied. And as he spoke, a large doe emerged from some bushes near the front gate and nosed around for something to eat.

"Do you have an aviation radio?" Stone asked.

Rawls rummaged around in a box and came up with a small radio and a charger, then plugged it in.

"Set it for 122.9," Stone said. "Lance's chopper is in the neighborhood." He picked up the radio. "Chopper, chopper, this is Barrington."

"This is Chopper One. I just cleared the hospital pad. What do you need?"

"Low aerial surveillance of the area of a house on the west shore, facing west, with a dock. There's a burning boat moored there. We're looking for a bunch of armed men in black."

"I'll get back," the pilot said.

Stone readdressed his beef stew.

A few minutes later, the radio came to life. "Barrington, Chopper One."

"I hear you."

"I'm off your dock. What the hell happened to that boat?"

"RPG."

"Oh, well."

"What do you see?"

"I just flushed a deer; she's moving south along the road. Uh-oh, SUV coming the other way, fast."

"Tell me more about the SUV."

"Oh, shit! It hit the deer! What . . . a . . . mess!"

"Do they need an ambulance?"

"I don't know. They're moving around. I see four men crawling out of the wreckage. One of them just shot the deer in the head."

"How are the men dressed?"

"Black combat gear. They look fully armored. Also assault weapons."

"Keep them in sight and report."

"Okay, they're walking up the road — scrub that, limping up the road. I'd say they're pissed off."

Stone turned to Rawls. "You hear that?"

"Every word," Rawls said. "Time to start shooting guns at them."

57

Stone checked out his H&K machine gun and tucked the aviation radio into his jacket's breast pocket with the antenna protruding.

"What do you want me to do?" Dino asked.

"Ed and I are going out to greet the four men limping up the road, so you'll be vulnerable from the north and east. Ed, do you have another aviation radio?"

Rawls rummaged around and came up with an older, larger one than before. He plugged it into the charger and dialed in the local frequency. "You can talk both to us and the chopper on this," he said to Dino. "Sally's had a lot of deer stalking experience in Scotland, courtesy of her father and late husband. She's got a Remington 30.06 with a scope; she's your artillery." He showed Dino how to manipulate the images from the outside cameras. "Give us a call if somebody's sneaking up on us, though the chopper will probably spot them first."

"Gotcha," Dino said. "Head off, and I'll watch you on TV."

Ed turned toward Stone. "I'm going to run across the drive to the gatepost. You cover me, then I'll cover you when you cross."

"Let's go," Stone said.

Ed cracked the side door, looked around, then broke for the gatepost on the other side of the driveway. He got there without being shot at, looked around and waved Stone across, then set up to cover him.

Stone ran across as fast as he could and settled behind the stacked stone pillar.

"The log across the drive will slow them down," Ed said. "When they're climbing over it would be a good time to kill them."

Stone nodded. He had no qualms about shooting to kill, after what these people had done to Rocky. He saw the top of somebody's head behind a bush, just the other side of the log. "Ready on the right," he said.

"Give me the first shot," Ed said. "Your weapon is better for close work."

"Right."

Ed unfolded a bipod from his assault rifle, set it on the stone pillar, and took careful aim. "One more step," he said.

367

Stone tensed as he saw a head pop up from behind the log, then as it exploded in a cloud of gore. "Good shot," he said, gulping.

"You're not going to toss your cookies, are you?" Ed asked.

"I might. What's it to you?"

"Let's advance, while they're figuring out what happened to their guy. You take the left, stop at the log."

The two of them split up and ran up the drive, hitting the dirt at the log.

"Don't stick your head up," Rawls said. "Remember what happened to the last guy who did that."

"Don't worry."

Ed produced a cardboard periscope from a pocket and unfolded it.

"Hang on a second," Stone said, bringing out the radio. "Chopper One."

"I hear ya. Nice head shot a minute ago."

"Can you see the other three?"

"Two across the main road, behind a large boulder. Don't move, until I find the other guy." There was a pause, then: "Got him. He's on your side of the road, behind another boulder, peeking out. You got a lot of boulders on this island."

"Yes, we do. Can I pop up for a second, without losing my head?"

"Maybe. It'll be the first boulder you see on your side of the road."

Stone popped up for about a second and took a mental photograph of what he saw. "All I saw was the boulder."

"He's still behind it, with a heavy rifle, something like a BAR."

"Swell." Stone put his weapon on full auto. "Ed, fire a couple of rounds at the guys across the road, to keep their heads down."

"Here you are," Ed said, squeezing off three or four rapid rounds.

Stone got the H&K into position, then stood up and waited. No sign of the man behind the rock.

"He's still there," the pilot radioed. "Getting ready to stand up."

Stone aimed six inches above the rock, and when the man stood, he squeezed off a burst, then disappeared behind his own rock.

"Target down, but moving," the pilot said. "His cap is off, and I see blood. I think you creased him."

"Go finish him off, Stone. I'll keep the others' heads down," Rawls said.

Stone unsnapped the keep on his shoulder holster, stood up, and ran toward the rock, maybe thirty yards away. He heard Ed fire a burst behind him, then he moved left, looking for his man. He ran right up to the boulder and looked over it. A man was sitting cross-legged on the ground, pressing his cap to a head wound.

"Sit still, or I'll blow the rest of your head off," Stone said. "Where's Gromyko?"

"Fuck you," the man said.

Stone pulled the 9mm from its holster, racked the slide, and shot him in the head. "Two down," he said into the radio, then he occupied the dead man's position behind the rock, which was sheltering him from the two across the road.

Suddenly, the two men stood up, one looking at him, the other at Rawls, and they began to sprint toward the log. Stone fired a low, sweeping burst and cut one of them down. The other was stopped by a bullet to the chest. "One down," he shouted. "Careful, the other guy is wearing a vest!" The man was partly sheltered behind his partner, and Stone didn't have a good shot. "He's yours, Ed!"

58

Stone kept the machine gun pointing at the downed man, as Ed ran across the road and kicked an assault rifle away from him, then took his sidearm out of a waist holster and threw it down the road a ways.

Stone ran up and did the same to the man he had shot, who seemed to have a single wound below his right knee. "I've got a live one. How about you?"

"He's a little alive," Ed replied, poking at him with his rifle barrel.

Stone walked over and tossed his man's weapon away. The man looked up at him with what seemed to be a combination of fear and hatred. "I've got time to put a tourniquet on that leg before you bleed to death," Stone said to the man. "If you talk fast. Where's Gromyko?"

"I don't know," the man said.

"I just killed your buddy over there for an incomplete answer to that question. Last chance: Where's the Greek?"

"Up that road behind you," the man said. "I don't know how far. He's in an armored Humvee."

"How did you get that thing onto the island?"

"We hired an old landing craft in Camden and put three vehicles ashore last night."

"What's the third vehicle?"

"An armored Range Rover. We had another, but we hit a deer. It's trashed." Stone held the machine gun pointed at his head, then bent over, pulled the cloth belt from the man's field jacket, and tossed it to him. "Get that on your leg." The man sat up and did as he was told.

"Did you get all that, Ed?" Stone asked.

"Yes, and a good thing, too; mine just died." He fired a shot into the man's head. "Just making sure."

Stone heard a vehicle approaching from the north and looked up in time to see a Range Rover approaching. He dragged the wounded man across the road and hid them both behind the boulder.

"I'm going back to the house!" Rawls cried. "Be right back, hold the fort!"

The radio in Stone's pocked cracked.

"This is Chopper One."

"I hear you."

"Two vehicles approaching from the north, an SUV and what looks like a larger vehicle."

"Do you have any arms aboard your chopper?" Stone asked.

"I've got a .45 on my belt. That's it."

"I could use a cannon," Stone said.

"I'm fresh out of cannons," the pilot replied. "All I've got are eyes. Both vehicles have stopped, and four men are getting out of the Range Rover with rifles. They can't see you behind the boulder. I think."

"Dino," Stone said. "If you can hear me, come up the drive with the heaviest weapons you've got. Watch out for Rawls. He's on the way to you. Don't startle him, or he'll shoot you." He released the talk button but heard no response. "Dino, do you read?" Nothing. "Dino?" Still nothing.

"Looks like you're in the shit," the wounded man on the ground said.

Stone wished he had kept the man's rifle. "If you make a sound to warn them we're here, you'll get my first bullet in your head," he said to the man. He could hear the tramp of boots on the road now, but he wasn't about to stick his head up.

"There's Pete over there," one of them said. "I don't see Art, do you?"

"Nope, but . . ." he said something Stone

couldn't make out. Stone's best guess was that he had seen the blood trail left by the wounded man at his side.

Suddenly his charge started yelling. "It's Art, Charlie, behind the . . ."

Stone shot him in the head with his handgun, then popped up for a second to see the two closest men, who were looking around for the source of the noise. Stone got to one knee, sighted quickly, and emptied the weapon in their direction. He ducked down again, popped out the empty magazine, and shoved another into the weapon. He popped up again. One man was writhing in the road, but the other had disappeared. Stone's best guess was behind his former boulder.

He spoke into the radio. "Dino, Ed? Anybody there?"

Nothing.

"If you can hear me, one down in the road but alive and the other maybe behind the boulder where I shot the other guy." Nothing. Why was he all alone? "Chopper, do you read?"

Nothing. He looked down at the radio and saw a small red light, flashing. "Insufficient charge," he said aloud to himself, "and I don't have another battery."

He took another look up the road and saw

two men dragging a third toward the Range Rover. He stood up, aimed just below them and emptied the magazine, walking his sightline up the road. He saw a headlamp explode on the Range Rover, then realized that both front doors had opened. The doors would be armored, giving them shelter. Stone looked up to see the chopper pass almost overhead, the pilot leaning out and waving at him. Stone pointed to his own ear and shook his head. The pilot nodded, then turned back toward the house.

Stone ran across the road and vaulted over the log gate. He heard firing from up the road, and bullets tearing into the log. Where the hell was everybody? He still had two more full magazines, so he reloaded and made a decision. He had to try for the house, before the Range Rover got here.

He stood up and started running.

59

Stone ran for the porch and through the side door, hardly slowing down. He closed the door behind him and looked around. "Hello? Anybody here?" Nothing.

He walked over to where the charger was plugged in and found a battery in it; the second radio was gone. He exchanged his dead battery for the good one, reloaded his gun belt with magazines for the machine gun, and pocketed some 9mm ones for his pistol. Where could they have gone?

He walked into the living room and looked out the front windows, down to the dock. Only a wisp of smoke was rising from the wreckage now, and there was no one in sight. He picked up the radio. "Chopper One, Barrington."

There was a lot of static and a broken transmission. Stone got only one word: "refuel." He hoped the man was in Rockland for that, not headed back north. Stone got the joystick controller and checked the outside cameras. Nothing was moving on any camera. He stopped and went left a few feet. Except one armored Humvee. It was coming down the road from the north, and there was a .50-caliber machine gun mounted on the rear open bay, manned by a character in the usual black body armor. The vehicle swung wide to the left, then turned back until it was ninety degrees to the big log gate.

He can't climb over it, Stone said to himself. He doesn't have enough road clearance. What's he going to do now?

He got a quick answer. The Humvee rolled forward until its steel-beam front bumper was hard against the log, then he heard the engine start to slowly rev.

That will never work, Stone said. Not even with four-wheel drive.

There was a shifting noise and the Humvee tried again. There was a groaning sound to be heard now, as if the vehicle was trying to break the log in two. Instead, the hinges fastening the log to a thick post began to shear their bolts.

"Oh, shit," Stone said aloud. Stone looked around the rooms for a heavier weapon than his machine gun. Ed said he'd used a rocket launcher on the boat. Where the hell is it?

The best he could do was a 12-gauge riot gun, and that wasn't going to work. He looked for the Remington deer rifle that Ed had spoken of, and that was gone, too.

The Humvee redoubled its efforts, and the log began to move, sliding slowly across the paved drive. The opening it left was widening, and in another minute, the vehicle would be able to just drive through it.

Stone picked up the radio. "Chopper One, Barrington. Do you read?"

"I read," a scratchy voice came back. "I needed fuel from Rockland. Be with you in a few minutes."

"Faster, please. I've got what amounts to a tank coming at me, and I can't look at it without catching lots of .50-caliber rounds."

"Coming as fast as I can."

The Humvee nosed the log out of its way and lumbered on, toward the house. The mounted machine gun began firing into the house, hammering against the steel shutters, penetrating some of them. Stone hit the floor and hugged it. Those were armor-piercing rounds, he figured.

He heard the Humvee come to a squeaky halt, and the engine shut down. Then came a voice over a bullhorn. "Everybody in the house outside now, or I'll reduce the building to kindling wood and kill everyone inside."

That was not an inviting choice, Stone thought. He raised his head and shouted, "Can you hear me?"

"Yes," the voice said. "Come outside, all of you."

"I'm alone," Stone answered. "Nobody here but me."

"All right, *you* come outside, unarmed. No rifle, no handgun, nothing. Or you can die there. No difference to me."

"All right," Stone yelled, "I'll come outside. Don't shoot me."

"If you're not armed, I've no reason to shoot you."

"I'm coming." Stone got to his feet, opened the door, and tossed the machine gun out into the driveway, followed by his handgun. "That's everything I've got." He peeked out the door, then drew back quickly.

"Don't be shy; come on out."

Stone spoke into the radio. "I have to go outside. Make some sort of ruckus, if you can do it without being shot down."

No response. Stone tested the waters with one foot outside.

"Keep coming!"

Stone walked out onto the porch and into

the driveway. The right passenger door of the Humvee opened, and somebody got out, using the door for shelter. Stone could see his legs, up to the knee. "Who are you?" he asked.

"Who do you think?" the man asked, stepping from behind the door. Not an inch of him was exposed. He wore thick gloves, body armor, and a combat helmet with a face mask.

"I want Gromyko," Stone said. "I want the Greek."

"I am the Greek," the man said.

"You're not the Greek. I know the Greek. Come on," Stone said, "take the fucking mask off, so I'll know who you are."

"You want to see the man who kills you?"

"Yes, I want to see the man who thinks he has the balls to kill me." He wished he could look around, because he thought he must have help out there somewhere. He heard the helicopter for the first time.

"All right," the man said. He leaned his assault rifle against the vehicle, reached up, unbuckled his chin strap, and shucked off the mask and helmet. It was the Greek.

Stone reached his pocket and pressed the talk button. "If anybody's there, please shoot the son of a bitch now. The machine gunner, too."

"Get your hand away from your pocket," Gromyko shouted.

Stone complied. "Tell you what, why don't we do this with knives? Mano a mano."

Gromyko smiled. "It would be my pleasure."

"Without the body armor," Stone said. Somebody please shoot.

Gromyko began unbuckling things, and Stone took off his shirt, exposing bare flesh. He wondered if Gromyko had ever been in a knife fight. He knew that he, himself, had not. He found the knife on his belt and pulled it.

Gromyko was ahead of him. He took two steps forward and stopped. "Come to me," he said.

Stone measured the distance between himself and his discarded machine gun, lying in the driveway. About ten feet, and the Greek was another thirty. Why had he thrown it so far? He took a couple of steps closer to it, and brought his knife up.

Gromyko produced a much larger knife and laughed. "I'm going to cut your head off," he said, conversationally.

Oh, all right, Stone thought, taking another step.

As he did, there were two quick noises in succession: one that knocked Gromyko down, and another that blew up the Humvee and knocked Stone backward, off his feet.

Stone lay on his back and looked at the sky, then his eyes began filling with blood.

"Talk to me, Stone," Rawls said.

60

Rawls pulled Stone into a sitting position. "I'm sorry about the RPG," he said. "You've taken some shrapnel."

"Get me on my feet," Stone managed to say. He struggled to stand up, with Rawls's help, found a handkerchief and wiped some of the blood off his face. Hanging on to Ed, he staggered forward toward the Greek, stopping to bend over and retrieve his pistol.

The Greek was holding a hand to his neck, trying to stanch the flow of blood. He was smiling at Stone.

"Don't die," Stone said.

"You want me to live?"

"No, I want to kill you myself."

Gromyko struggled to one elbow, while holding his other hand to the wound. "I will kill you with my fingers," he said.

"I don't think so." Stone pointed the weapon at him and fired a round, which missed and struck the ground behind him.

"You're a little wobbly," Ed said. "You want me to do that for you?"

"No, thanks, I'd rather do it myself."

The Greek got into a sitting position. "Your girlfriend is dead," he said, still grinning. "One of my men killed her in the hospital about an hour ago. Her brains went everywhere."

"Now," Stone said, moving forward and shaking off Rawls. "No more time." He took aim from about six feet, squeezed the trigger, and the top of Gromyko's head disappeared.

"Nice shot," Rawls said, catching Stone again before he could fall. "Come into the house. Let's get you seen to."

Stone struggled into the house and collapsed into a chair, while Rawls located a first-aid kit in a tin suitcase.

Ed got a fistful of gauze pads and started dabbing the blood off Stone's face, chest, and arms.

"Did you hear what he said before he died?" Stone asked.

"No."

"He said Rocky was dead, that one of his men killed her at the hospital."

"That's bullshit. She's too well-guarded."

Sally came into the room and set down her deer rifle. "I got the bastard," she said.

"That was you?"

"It was," Rawls answered for her. "First shot. From a helicopter, by God. It was a beautiful thing."

"I liked the effect," Stone said. "Also, the part about saving my life. That was fun."

"Ed got the Humvee with the RPG."

"It was the only thing on the island that would have stopped that thing," Ed said, "and I only had the one round." Ed applied some skin-colored tape to several places on Stone's face. "I don't think you'll need stitches, but you may not be quite as pretty as before."

"The scars will give him character," Sally said.

"Where's the chopper?" Stone asked. "I want to see Rocky."

"On the front lawn," Sally replied. "Plenty of fuel."

Stone's phone rang. He dug it out and looked at the caller ID: Krause. "Oh, God," he said. "It's her doctor, with the news." Reluctantly, he pressed the button. "Yes?"

"It's Paul Krause," the doctor said. "With news."

"I heard," Stone replied.

"How?"

"The Greek told me."

"I'll tell you again. Rocky began coming

385

to ten minutes ago, and she's talking a little," Krause said. "Hold on, she wants to speak to you."

Stone found that he had been holding his breath, and he let it all out.

"Stone?" a weak voice said.

"Hello, Rocky," he said. "Welcome back."

Krause took the phone back. "That's all she can manage for a bit."

"Tell her I'm choppering in," Stone said.

"I'll do that."

Rawls took the phone from Stone. "Doctor?"

"Yes?"

"Our boy Stone needs some medical attention when he gets there."

"It's what we do," Krause said, then hung up.

"Do you think you can get me into the chopper?" Stone asked.

"Dino's already aboard. It will take us all there."

Rawls hung Stone's shirt on his shoulders and tied the sleeves in a loose knot. Stone got to his feet and, leaning on Sally, hobbled out to the waiting aircraft.

The engines started.

AUTHOR'S NOTE

I am happy to hear from readers, but you should know that if you write to me in care of my publisher, three to six months will pass before I receive your letter, and when it finally arrives it will be one among many, and I will not be able to reply.

However, if you have access to the Internet, you may visit my website at www.stuart woods.com, where there is a button for sending me e-mail. So far, I have been able to reply to all my e-mail, and I will continue to try to do so.

Remember: e-mail, reply; snail mail, no reply.

When you e-mail, please do not send attachments, as I never open these. They can take twenty minutes to download, and they often contain viruses.

Please do not place me on your mailing lists for funny stories, prayers, political causes, charitable fund-raising, petitions, or sentimental claptrap. I get enough of that from people I already know. Generally speaking, when I get e-mail addressed to a large number of people, I immediately delete it without reading it.

Please do not send me your ideas for a book, as I have a policy of writing only what I myself invent. If you send me story ideas, I will immediately delete them without reading them. If you have a good idea for a book, write it yourself, but I will not be able to advise you on how to get it published. Buy a copy of *Writer's Market* at any bookstore; that will tell you how.

Anyone with a request concerning events or appearances may e-mail it to me or send it to: Putnam Publicity Department, Penguin Random House LLC, 1745 Broadway, New York, NY 10019.

Those ambitious folk who wish to buy film, dramatic, or television rights to my books should contact Matthew Snyder, Creative Artists Agency, 2000 Avenue of the Stars, Los Angeles, CA 90067.

Those who wish to make offers for rights of a literary nature should contact Anne Sibbald, Janklow & Nesbit, 285 Madison Avenue, 21st Floor, New York, NY 10017. (Note: This is not an invitation for you to send her your manuscript or to solicit her

388

to be your agent.)

If you want to know if I will be signing books in your city, please visit my website, www.stuartwoods.com, where the tour schedule will be published a month or so in advance. If you wish me to do a book signing in your locality, ask your favorite bookseller to contact his Penguin representative or the Penguin publicity department with the request.

If you find typographical or editorial errors in my book and feel an irresistible urge to tell someone, please write to Sara Minnich at Penguin's address above. Do not e-mail your discoveries to me, as I will already have learned about them from others.

All the novels are still in print in paperback and can be found at or ordered from any bookstore. If you wish to obtain hardcover copies of earlier novels or of the two nonfiction books, a good used-book store or one of the online bookstores can help you find them. Otherwise, you will have to go to a great many garage sales.

ABOUT THE AUTHOR

Stuart Woods is the author of more than eighty novels, including the #1 *New York Times*-bestselling Stone Barrington series. He is a native of Georgia and began his writing career in the advertising industry. *Chiefs,* his debut in 1981, won the Edgar Award. An avid sailor and pilot, Woods lives in Florida, Maine, and New Mexico.

The employees of Thorndike Press hope you have enjoyed this Large Print book. All our Thorndike, Wheeler, and Kennebec Large Print titles are designed for easy reading, and all our books are made to last. Other Thorndike Press Large Print books are available at your library, through selected bookstores, or directly from us.

For information about titles, please call:
(800) 223-1244

or visit our website at:
gale.com/thorndike

To share your comments, please write:
Publisher
Thorndike Press
10 Water St., Suite 310
Waterville, ME 04901